New Aesop Fables for Children
Volumes 1-5

(Bilingual Version – Chinese and English)

Written by Robert W. Long

Edited/Translated by Rong Zhang

Art

The manga is from Hokusai, 1997 Master Graphique CD-Rom Anthology. All rights reserved.

First Edition: ©Robert Long 2006
Second Edition [Bilingual Version]: May, 2022
ISBN: 9798831483734

Preface

In 620 BC, Aesop was born as a slave and was owned by two masters, the latter of whom freed him due to his wit and learning. In time, Aesop raised himself to a position of high renown, and he began to travel through many countries. He met with philosophers, Phadedo, Menippus, and Epictetus, along with such sages as Solon and Thales when he went to the court of Croesus. Croesus was so pleased by him that he was hired as a public official and as a diplomat. It was during one of the ambassadorial missions to Delphi that Aesop was killed—his death seemed to be avenged by a series of calamities.

Aesop's travels, most likely, allowed him to become acquainted with all kinds of virtues and vices. Aesop wrote his fables to provide instruction and guidance for all mankind; likewise, these fables were written for the same purpose, particularly as people today are growing up without a moral compass to guide them through complex social issues. As many of the characters in these fables represent common hopes, ideals, goals and shortcomings that shape society today, it is my hope that people, young and old, can learn and discuss the benefits of virtues, and the consequences of vices, so that they can develop the insight to more effectively shape their own lives and society in a more meaningful way. It's not easy trying to expand on the fables of Aesop, for their charm, wisdom, humor, and characters transcend time, and speak to us as clearly as they did so long ago. It was, no doubt, because of Aesop's hard background that he was able to see the 'lessons of life' that so many others miss.

These fables I believe particularly appeal to Chinese parents with young children for bedtime stories because they can teach their children the wisdom they need in their future life. It is also a valuable book to help the children to develop their bilingual skills in both English and Chinese while enjoying these interesting stories. "Taking It a Step Further – Moral Prompts" provides questions for readers to think about further. We suggest that parents have further discussions with their children to help them think more creatively. Learners of Chinese can also practice speaking through retelling of these fables. We sincerely hope that you will have a fruitful and relaxing experience with our book.

Robert W. Long III

Rong Zhang

February, 2022

Table of Contents

Volume 1

Volume 2

Volume 3

Volume 4

Volume 5

Fable 1 The Donkey and the Crickets

A donkey heard some crickets chirping in the bushes. He thought the sound was beautiful. He asked the crickets, "What food do you eat? Why do you sing so well?"

"Oh, Mr. Donkey, we eat only the morning dew. It also keeps us beautiful," replied the crickets.

The donkey was shocked! "Dew?! Dew?! That's crazy! That's too hard just to sound good. I'll just eat my corn and oatmeal, because I like them. Thank you very much!"

Moral: Some things cost too much to achieve.

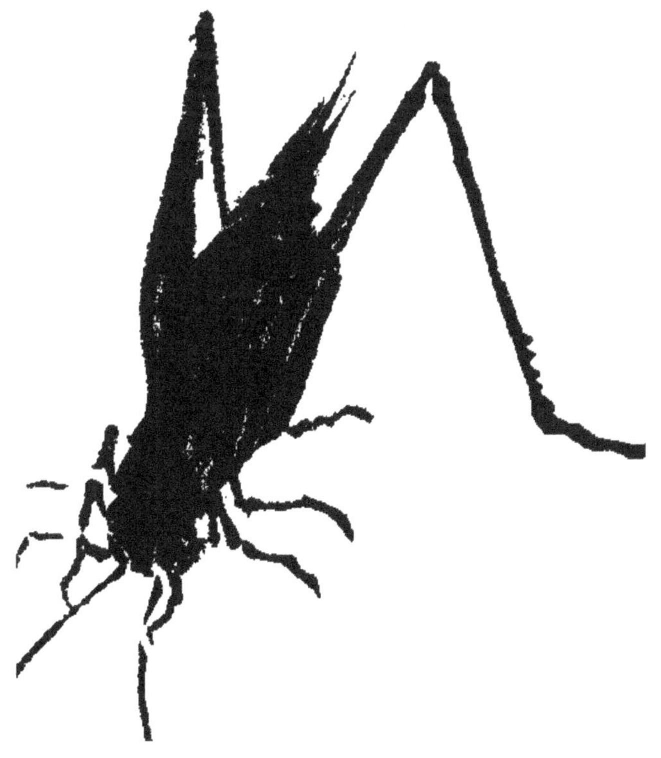

寓言1　驴和蟋蟀

一只驴听到一些蟋蟀在灌木丛中唧唧地叫。他觉得那个声音太美妙了，于是问蟋蟀们，"你们吃什么食物？为什么你们唱歌这么好听？"

"哦，驴先生，我们只是吃晨露。他也让我们保持美丽。"蟋蟀们回答。

驴很惊讶，说："露水？露水？不可思议啊！想要美妙的声音，太难了！我还是吃玉米和燕麦吧，因为我喜欢。谢谢！"

寓意：有些事情需要付出太多才能获得。

Taking It a Step Further——Moral Prompts

*Try to name five things from your experience that "cost too much."

*What is another good moral for this fable?

Fable 2 Those Delicious Grapes

Three men were walking down a country road. They saw some grapes. One big bunch of grapes was really beautiful. The grapes were as big as a cow's eyes and as purple as midnight. They glistened with the morning dew.

The first man said, "These grapes will be a fine breakfast." The second man said, "No, these grapes will be a fine wine." The third man said, "No, they will be a fine gift." The three men started to fight loudly. The owner of the grapes heard them and chased them away.

Moral: Fighting will never get you the things you want.

寓言2　　美味的葡萄

三个人走在乡间的小路上。他们看见一些葡萄，其中一串特别漂亮。

那些葡萄像牛的眼睛一样颗粒饱满，像午夜的天色一样呈紫色。他们在晨露中闪着光亮。

第一个人说，"这些葡萄可以成为美味的早餐。"

第二个人说，"不，这些葡萄可以成为醇香的美酒。"

第三个人说，"不，他们可以成为上好的礼物。"

这三个人开始大声争吵。葡萄的主人听到了，于是把他们撵走。

寓意：争吵永远不会让你拥有想要的东西。

Taking It a Step Further——Moral Prompts

*What kinds of things have you seen people fight over?

*What is another good moral for this fable?

Fable 3 The Dog's Reflection

A dog stole a steak from a trash can. The dog thought it was very clever. It raced away with the steak in its mouth.

Finally it came to a bridge. There it felt safe enough to stop. The dog put down the steak to catch its breath. It noticed its re-flection in the river.

"I am really a good-looking dog," it said in a loud voice. This woke another dog that was sleeping on the bridge. The other dog saw the steak on the road. It picked up the steak and raced off with it. The first dog could only look at itself in the river.

Moral: Vanity will cost you.

寓言3   狗的影子

一只狗从一个垃圾箱里偷了一块牛排。狗觉得自己很聪明。他把牛排衔在嘴里跑开了。

最后，狗来到了一座桥。他觉得很安全了，才停下来，把牛排放下来喘气。他看到了自己在河里的影子。

"我真是一只好看的狗。"他大声说。

这只狗的声音叫醒了另一只在桥上睡觉的狗，他也看到了路上的牛排。于是他叼起牛排就跑了。第一只狗继续欣赏着他在河里的影子。

寓意：自负让你付出代价。

Taking It a Step Further——Moral Prompts

*Which group of people do you think are the vainest?

*What is more important: inner beauty or outer beauty?

Fable 4 The Ants and the Cricket

The ants were spending their autumn, as usual, storing up food. A cricket passed by jumping, singing, and dancing. The ants called out, "Hey cricket, don't you think you should store up some food for the winter?"

"Store up some food?" the cricket asked. "Why should I do that!? I have friends, you know. They will take care of me!" The ants went back to work. However, they often laughed at the cricket. They repeated what he said. "I have friends, you know," they laughed. "What a fool!"

Winter and snow came. Sometimes the ants would look out of their anthills. They looked for the frozen cricket. They wanted to eat him! But every time, they saw that that the cricket was warm and safe. He was singing and dancing in the homes of his friends.

Moral: Those who are good at making friends don't go hungry.

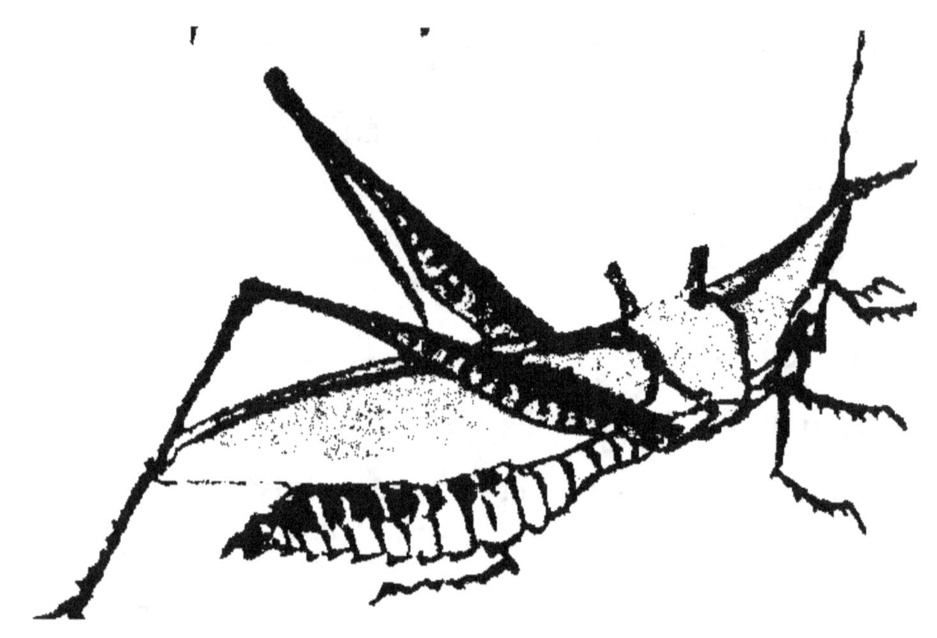

寓言4　　　蚂蚁和蟋蟀

蚂蚁们如往常的秋天一样，在储备食物。一只蟋蟀蹦跳着从旁边经过，载歌载舞。蚂蚁们大声喊，〝喂，蟋蟀，你难道不应该为冬天储备一些食物吗？〞

〝储备食物？〞蟋蟀问。〝我有必要自己做吗？你知道，我有朋友。他们会照顾我！〞蚂蚁们回去工作了。可是他们经常嘲笑蟋蟀，重复着他的话，〝你知道，我有朋友。〞他们嘲笑他，〝真是个傻瓜！〞

冬天来了，下雪了。蚂蚁们有时候从蚁冢向外望，想找到冻僵了的蟋蟀，把他吃掉。可是每次，他们都看到蟋蟀在朋友们的家里，又唱又跳，温暖安全。

寓意：善于交朋友的人不会没饭吃。

Taking It a Step Further——Moral Prompts

*Are you good at making new friends?

*What is another good moral for this fable?

Fable 5 The Bear and the Fox

A bear boasted about its strength to all of the animals in the forest. A fox heard his boasting and called out,

"Yes, but if you are so strong, why do you always run away from men? Your strength is no match for their guns!" The bear then chased the fox deep into the forest.

Moral: No one likes a critic.

寓言 5熊和狐狸

一只熊和森林里的所有动物炫耀自己力大无比。一只狐狸听到了，大声喊到，〝是这样的。可是如果你果真强壮，为什么总是躲避人类？你的力气比不过他们的枪。〞熊马上开始追逐狐狸进了树林里。

寓意：没有人喜欢被品头论足。

Taking It a Step Further——Moral Prompts

*Does anyone criticize you?

*Does criticism really help anyone to change?

Fable 6 The Man Bitten by a Dog

A man saw his friend walking a very big, very ugly dog. The friend called out and wanted to chat, but the man stayed far away. He was afraid the dog would bite him. After a short chat, the man walked on. He soon saw another friend with a pretty little poodle. He greeted his friend and said, "What a cute dog you have. What's its name?" The man reached down to pet the dog, but the dog jumped up and bit him on the hand.

Moral: The small and pretty can be as dangerous as the large and ugly.

寓言 6　　被狗吃掉的人

一个人看见他的朋友在遛一只体型巨大，长相丑陋的狗。朋友大声喊，想和他聊天。可是那个人远远躲开。他害怕狗会咬他。

简短地聊了几句，这个人继续往前走。他看到另一个朋友带着一只非常漂亮的小型贵宾犬。

他打招呼说，＂你的狗太可爱了！他叫什么名字？＂

这个人俯下身去抚摸小狗，可是小狗跳起来，咬了他的手。

寓意：又小又可爱的东西也会和又大又丑陋的一样危险（不能以貌取人）。

Taking It a Step Further——Moral Prompts

*Name a small creature that is very dangerous?
*Which kind of animals are you afraid of and why?

Fable 7 The Donkey and the Children

A donkey saw its owner's children playing in the yard. They were splashing water and running around in circles. The owner laughed and laughed. So the donkey decided to do the same thing. He splashed in the water and ran around in circles. But the donkey was very surprised. The owner didn't laugh. He just beat the donkey and said, "Stop that, you bad donkey!"

Moral: Don't try to be something you are not.

寓言 7　　驴和孩子们

一只驴看到他的主人的孩子们在院子里玩耍。他们正在戏水，绕圈儿奔跑。主人笑意盈盈。于是驴也决定做同样的事情。

他在水里啪嗒啪嗒地玩耍，一圈圈奔跑。可是驴很惊讶，主人没有笑。他只是打了驴，说到，＂快停止吧。你这只愚蠢的驴！＂

寓意：不要试图模仿别人。

Taking It a Step Further——Moral Prompts

*Should the donkey be blamed for trying to be something it is not?

*What is another good moral for this fable?

Fable 8 The Fisherman and His Net

Once, a fisherman made a very special net. He thought he could get a great catch. He spent many months sewing each spot and testing its strength. Finally it was ready. He took the net out to sea to his favorite spot and tossed it out.

He began to laugh and sing, thinking about all the fish he would catch. But as he started to bring in the net, the logs and garbage in the sea tore huge holes in it. The net was useless.

Moral: Watch where you put your treasures.

寓言8　　渔夫和渔网

有一次，渔夫制作了一个非常特殊的渔网。他想自己一定可以捕获很多鱼。

他花了很多时间编制网结，测试他的强度。

最后渔网终于制成了。他带着渔网出海到最中意的地点，撒网。他开始欢笑，唱歌，想着他可能捕获的鱼。

可是在他开始收网的时候，海里的木头和垃圾把渔网撕开了一个大洞。渔网变成了废物。

寓意：看护好你的宝物。

Taking It a Step Further——Moral Prompts

*There are many kinds of treasures in this world: money, gold, silver, stocks, bonds, travels, objects, antiques, etc. What kind of treasure is the most valuable and long-lasting?

*Are people today too focused on accumulating "treasures"?

Fable 9 The Crab and its Mother

A mother crab said to her son, "Now, if you want to grow up, you will have to watch out for the birds. They like to eat us. If you see one swooping down at you, you had better run to the water. Also, if you see any humans—they are giants on two long legs—you had better run to the water, too. They like to eat us, too. And when you are in the water, watch out for large fish. They like to eat us, too. Now, do you have any questions?"

Her son said, "My gosh, if death comes from the sky, and from the ground, and is in the sea, then where can I find safety?

"Son, the only place you will find safety is in your eyes, head, and legs. I think it is the same with all creatures though. Don't worry about it."

Moral: A bad situation isn't so bad if you remember your abilities.

寓言 9　　螃蟹和他的妈妈

一只螃蟹妈妈对他的儿子说，＂现在，如果你想要长大，就必须小心鸟类。他们喜欢吃我们。如果你看到有一只在向我们俯冲过来，你最好钻到水里。同样，如果你看到任何人类—他们是长着两条长腿的巨人—你也最好钻到水里。他们也喜欢吃我们。你在水里的时候，要小心大鱼。他们也喜欢吃我们。你还有什么问题吗？＂

他的儿子回答，＂我的天哪！如果死亡来自于天空，陆地和水里，在哪儿我才是安全的？＂

〝儿子，只有一个地方你才能获得安全，　就是运用你的眼睛，头脑和腿。我觉得这个也适用于所有生物。不用担心啊。〞

寓意：如果你还记得自己的能力，糟糕的情况也不会太坏

（要依靠自己的能力去应对不利的情况。）

Taking It a Step Further——Moral Prompts

*In looking back at your life, can you describe a bad situation? Was it really that bad?

*What kind of abilities do you have?

Fable 10 The Mouse, the Frog, and the Hawk

Once there was a mouse who had always wanted to travel and see the world. He met a frog with the same idea. "Let's go and find some fun," the mouse suggested to his new friend. The two creatures were so small and slow, they didn't go very far or very fast. They saw a hawk flying in the sky. They had never seen a hawk before.

"Wow!" said the mouse. "Amazing!" answered the frog. "That's the best way to travel," added the mouse.

"Let's go with him," suggested the frog. Using some flags and fires, the two caught the attention of the hawk. The hawk then flew down and ate the mouse and the frog.

Moral: The "slow" way is often safer than the "fast" way.

寓言 10　　老鼠，青蛙和老鹰

从前，有一只老鼠总是想要去旅行，看看世界。他遇到了一只青蛙和他有同样的想法。"让我们去寻找快乐吧。"老鼠对他的新朋友建议说。可是他们两个太小，又太慢，他们走不了很远，很快。他们看见一只老鹰在天上飞。他们以前从来没有见过老鹰。

"哇～！"老鼠说。

"太神奇了！"青蛙回答。

"那是最好的旅行方式。"老鼠接着说。

"让我们和他一起去。"青蛙建议说。他们用旗帜和火，终于吸引了老鹰的注意力。老鹰于是俯冲下来，把老鼠和青蛙吃掉了。

寓意：　慢的方法通常比快的更安全。

Taking It a Step Further——Moral Prompts

*Do you agree with this moral, that the fast way often is more dangerous than the "slow way"?

*Do you know about the original fable of Aesop concerning the mouse, frog and the hawk? What was the moral to this story?

Fable 11 The Dress

A long time ago, there was a woman who was famous for her good taste in clothing. She went to buy a beautiful, warm dress. She went from store to store, but she couldn't find a dress that was both stylish and warm.

Finally she came to a small corner store. She told her driver to stop. The storekeeper welcomed her and showed her many dresses. The woman was amazed. "Your store is so small, but your collection is endless," she said.

Finally, after four hours, she picked a beautiful blue wool dress and bought it. On the way out of the door, she tripped over a poor beggar who was sleeping in the cold. The woman started yelling and kicking the beggar. The storekeeper was so shocked! She ran to the woman, threw her money back at her, took back the dress, and said, "Only good people should wear good clothes! And you are not good enough for one of my dresses." Then she ran back into the store and locked the door.

Moral: It is better to BE good than to LOOK good.

寓言 11　　连衣裙

很久以前，有一个女人因为对着装很有品位而有名。她去买一件漂亮，暖和的连衣裙。

她走了一家又一家商店，可是她找不到一件又时髦又保暖的连衣裙。

最后，她来到一个拐角处的小店。她让司机停下车。店主很欢迎她，给她看了很多件连衣裙。这个女人很惊讶。〝你的商店很小，但是却有源源不断的货品。〞她说。在四个小时之后，她终于挑选了一件漂亮的蓝色羊毛连衣裙购买。

走出店外，她被一个在寒冷中睡觉的乞丐绊倒。这个女人开始叫喊，用脚踢乞丐。

店主非常震惊！她跑向那个女人，把钱扔给她，拿回了衣服。她说，〝只有善良的人才能穿漂亮衣服。你配不上我的任何一件连衣裙。〞然后，她跑回商店，关上了门。

寓意：　和漂亮的外表相比，善良更重要。

Taking It a Step Further——Moral Prompts

*Many rich people have very fine clothes, but do you think most rich people are "fine people"?

*What is another good moral for this fable?

Fable 12 The Two Sisters

Once there were two sisters. Sharon, the older sister, was very beautiful and charming. Joanne, the younger sister, was ugly and awkward. At home, guests liked to talk to Sharon. Joanne had to serve tea.

At school, the boys and the teachers were interested in Sharon. Joanne had to clean the blackboards and sweep the floors.

After school, the two sisters decided to work in the public library. Mr. Carsdill, the head librarian, interviewed both girls. He quickly decided their jobs. Joanne had to work at the front desk and check out books. Sharon became Mr. Carsdill's assistant. Her desk was next to Mr. Carsdill's desk. Joanne could meet with all the people in the library, make friends, and enjoy reading lots of the books. Sharon never understood her job. She just sat next to Mr. Carsdill.

Moral: Beauty can be a curse.

寓言 12　　两姐妹

从前，有两姐妹。莎仑是姐姐，特别漂亮，迷人。乔安妮是妹妹，丑陋，令人尴尬。在家里，客人们都喜欢和莎仑聊天。乔安妮只能上茶。

在学校，男孩子们和老师对莎仑感兴趣。乔安妮不得不擦黑板，擦地。

毕业以后，两姐妹决定在公共图书馆工作。图书馆馆长，卡斯蒂尔先生面试了两个姐妹。他很快给她们分配了工作。

乔安妮在前台工作，负责借书手续。莎仑成了卡斯蒂尔先生的助手。她的书桌在卡斯蒂尔先生的旁边。

乔安妮可以见到图书馆里的每个人，交朋友，享受读书的乐趣。莎仑从来不懂乔安妮的工作。她只是坐在卡斯蒂尔先生的旁边。

寓意： 漂亮有时是一个诅咒。

Taking It a Step Further——Moral Prompts

*If you could make yourself "ten times more attractive," would this be a very good thing for your life? What would change?

*In what other ways can beauty be a curse?

*Can you discuss what happened to ten beautiful movie stars that you know about?

Fable 13 Heavy Baggage

A long time ago all of the animals could talk to each other and were friends. The rabbits were the most talkative of all of the animals. One day, as the sky began to get dark and cloudy, a rabbit started running home along a mountain road. The rabbit soon passed a turtle. The turtle was also trying to find shelter from the storm. The rabbit was puzzled. "Why are you going so slowly? Why don't you go faster?" he asked.

"Oh," the turtle replied proudly, "Inside my shell, I have a food cupboard, a footstool, and a bed. I also have the best books and a few musical instruments. No other animal has anything like them."

"Hmm ...." said the rabbit. "I NEVER had those things. You are so lucky!"

"No, no, I'm not lucky, my friend," boasted the turtle, "I'm intelligent and hard working. I have money, a very GOOD education, and . ."

"Maybe you're right," interrupted the rabbit, "but I have to run. I don't want to get wet. Bye." And the rabbit ran home. The turtle was still walking slowly in the rain.

Moral: Humble people travel faster because they carry less baggage.

寓言 13　　沉重的行李

很久以前，所有的动物都是好朋友，可以互相交流。在所有的动物里，兔子是最健谈的。一天，当天空开始变暗，转阴，一只兔子开始沿着山路往家跑。这只兔子很快超过了一只乌龟。乌龟也在试图找一个地方躲避暴风雨。兔子很疑惑。"你为什么走那么慢？为什么不快走？"他他问。

"哦，"乌龟骄傲地回答，"在我的龟壳里，我有一个装食物的橱柜，一个脚凳和一张床。我还有最好的书和一些乐器。别的动物可没有这些。"

"嗯，"兔子说，"我从来没有那些东西。你可真幸运！"

"不，不，我不是幸运，我的朋友，"乌龟夸耀说，"我是聪明，勤奋。我有钱，受过很好的教育，还有。。。"

"你可能说对了，"兔子打断他，"可是我不得不快跑。我不想被淋湿。再见。"

兔子跑回了家。乌龟还在雨中缓慢地爬行。

寓意：　谦虚的人走得更快，因为他们轻装上阵。

Taking It a Step Further——Moral Prompts

*Do you consider yourself a humble person?

*Do you think having very few possessions throughout your life is a good idea?

Fable 14 Rennid. Rennid.

A fox had not eaten for a week. He was crazy with hunger and had almost no more hope. Then he saw a fat squirrel high up in a tree. The fox knew that squirrels like to talk. So the fox stood next to a big rock and yelled, "Olleh rennid!" The squirrel didn't even look up.

The fox called out again, louder, "Rennid olleh!" Without looking up, the squirrel replied, "Ol-leh yourself. Now, GO AWAY."

The fox walked back and forth. He was so hungry he couldn't stand it. But he knew that patience often brings rewards, so he calmly called out, "WON! WON. Nowd! Rennid! Rennid!

The squirrel looked up. He was quite annoyed at this noise. "WHAT?! WHAT? Speak up you fool. What did you win? WHAT? I'm busy, you know!" The fox began to jump up and down, pointing to the rock.

"Rennid. DOOG! DOOG! Won! Won," the fox shouted. The squirrel was now really annoyed and began to yell back, "I'm NO DOG. I am a SQUIRREL!

Are you BLIND?" But he was becoming more and more curious about the rock. The fox was so hungry he thought he was dying. He now began to jump up and down, bark, and pant.

"GNI-tast-doog. Y-TAST. Won! Won," he repeated again and again. The squirrel was really angry! "WHAT is Y-TAST? HUH? CAN'T YOU SPEAK RIGHT?" The squirrel slowly started to crawl down the branch so he could see better.

The fox didn't give up. He started to run in circles, barking at the rock, still pointing. He was very excited.

"RENNID! RENNID. NWOD. NWOD. WON!"

The squirrel didn't know what to do. The fox was very dangerous. But what was behind this rock? Quickly, the squirrel jumped from the branch over to the rock.

Right away, the fox jumped on the squirrel and ate him. The fox licked his lips and thought to himself, "I never knew talking backwards was such a good idea!"

Moral: Patience brings rewards.

寓言 14　　雷尼德！雷尼德！

一只狐狸已经一个星期没有吃饭了。他对饥饿感到疯狂，几乎完全失望。他看到了一只肥硕的松鼠高高在树上。狐狸知道松鼠喜欢说话，于是站在一块巨大岩石的旁边，大声喊，＂噢勒，雷尼德！＂松鼠甚至都没有抬头看。

狐狸又一次用更大的声音叫喊，〝雷尼德，噢勒！〞松鼠没有抬头，回答说，〝噢-勒-，狐狸先生，现在走开吧。〞

狐狸走来走去。他太饿了，不能再忍受。可是他知道耐心经常会带来回报，于是他冷静地大声说，〝赢了！赢了！雷尼德！雷尼德！〞

松鼠抬起头。他对于这个声音非常生气，〝什么？什么？说清楚，蠢蛋！你赢了什么？是什么？我很忙，你知道的！〞狐狸开始跳上跳下，指着岩石说。

〝雷尼德。DOOG！GOOG！赢了！赢了！〞狐狸大声喊。松鼠真地生气了，大声喊，〝我不是狗。我是松鼠！你瞎了吗？〞

但是他变得对岩石越来越感兴趣。狐狸太饿了，他觉得自己快死了。他开始跳来跳去，嘶喊着，喘着粗气。

〝GNI-tast-doog. Y-TAST。赢了！赢了！〞他一次又一次重复。松鼠变得愤怒，〝Y-TAST 是什么？你能不能说明白？〞

松鼠开始慢慢爬下低矮的树枝，他想看清楚。狐狸没有放弃。他开始转着圈儿跑，仍然指着岩石，兴奋地大声喊。

〝雷尼德！雷尼德！赢了！赢了！〞

松鼠不知道该怎么办了。狐狸很危险。可是岩石的后面到底有什么呢？于是，松鼠快速从树枝上跳到岩石上。狐狸立刻跳上去，吃掉了松鼠。狐狸舔着嘴唇，对自己说，〝我从来都没有想过，回话是这么好的主意！〞

寓意：　耐心会带来回报。

Taking It a Step Further——Moral Prompts

*Why are patient people smart?

*Are you very patient?

Fable 15 Cricket Concerts

Every night (except for the coldest nights of winter), the crickets around the world put on their night concert for all of the animals. Most of the cricket bands work together with together with no problems. However, one small band of crickets had many problems.

The worst problem was getting the crickets to come to practice. One night no one showed up. Jannie, the conductor, went to the homes of all the members. She stopped by Mimmie's home first. (Mimmie played the violin.) She knocked on the door many times. Finally Mimmie opened it.

"Why aren't you at the concert hall, Mimmie? It's time for our practice. Hurry up." Mimmie was dressed in a beautiful dress. She quickly replied, "Quiet please. I have very important friends here now. I can't come tonight. See you."

Jannie also learned that Wonnie, the bass section leader, was too busy to come. She had to take out the garbage. Lonnie, an- other violinist, also couldn't come. She was helping her children with their homework.

Jannie was worried. She visited five other band members. They said they were sick, on vacation, out shopping, or had to take care of grandparents. That night, a very tired Jannie went to bed. She thought, "Well, I tried. At least everyone had a good excuse."

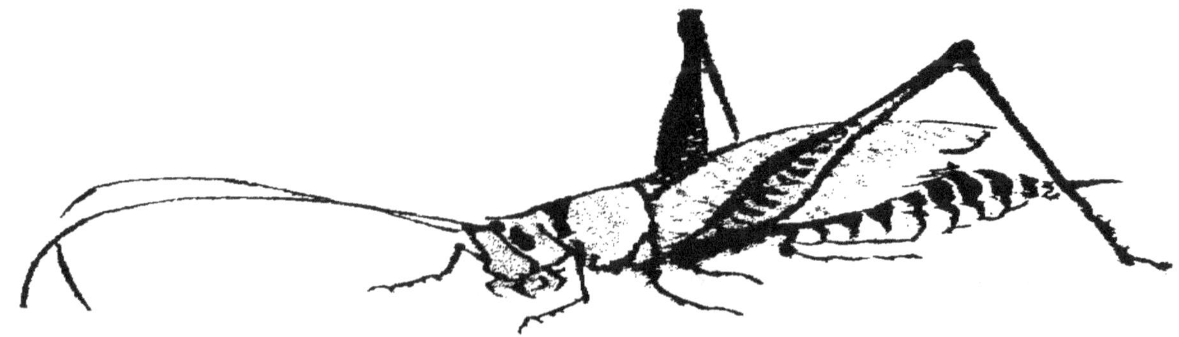

Moral: You do the things that you really want to do.

寓言 15　　蟋蟀音乐会

每个晚上(除了冬天里最冷的夜晚)，世界上蟋蟀会为了所有的动物，举行夜晚音乐会。

几乎所有的蟋蟀乐队一起合作，没有出现问题。可是，有一个小的蟋蟀乐队有很多麻烦。

最大的问题是怎样让蟋蟀们来练习。一天晚上，一只蟋蟀也没有来。乐队指挥，珍妮，去了每一个成员的家里。　她最先去了咪咪家（咪咪是小提琴手）。她敲门很多次，咪咪终于开门了。

〝你为什么没去音乐厅，咪咪？到我们练习的时间了。快去！〞咪咪穿着一件漂亮的连衣裙。她马上回答，〝请安静。有非常重要的朋友在我这里。今天晚上我去不了。再见。〞

珍妮后来知道，汪妮，低音部的领唱，太忙了，来不了。她需要扔垃圾。龙妮，另一位小提琴手也不能来。她在帮孩子们做作业。

珍妮很发愁。她又去了另外五个乐队成员的家。他们有的说病了，有的在度假，有的在外购物，有的要照顾祖父母。那天晚上，珍妮疲惫地上床睡觉。她想，〝好吧，我尽力了。至少每个人都有很好的理由。〞

寓意：　只管做自己想做的事情(不要在意结果)。

Taking It a Step Further——Moral Prompts

*What kinds of things do you want to do?

*What kinds of things are you forced to do?

Fable 16 Go Left, Turn Right

Some crows were pecking and searching through some garbage on a street corner. A man walked by. He was lost, so he asked the crows, "Do you know where the train station is?"

"Sure," replied a large crow named Jeb. "Go left, turn right, go straight."

"Thanks," smiled the man. He hurried away. The rest of the crows (Flaky, Jam, Crusty, Eggshell, and Pit) crowded around Jeb. They talked in the language of the crows.

Flaky: "English is so hard! What does 'train station' mean?"

Jeb: "I don't know. I just know, 'go left, turn right, go straight.'"

Jam: "But the man was happy."

Jeb: "Well, I've learned to keep it simple. People don't like difficult answers."

Crusty: "You are so smart, Jeb!"

Jeb: "And I learned to always say 'sure.' People don't like to hear 'no.'"

Eggshell: "You are so helpful, Jeb!"

Jeb: "Yes, I know. And I'm quick too. People want fast answers. Don't talk slow."

Pit: "You are so clever, Jeb. I didn't know that."

Jeb: "Yes—yes. I wish people were clever, too. That man just walked past all the free food on this corner!"

Moral: Vanity is misleading.

寓言 16　　往左走，向右拐

一些乌鸦在一个街角的垃圾堆里啄食，寻找。一个男人经过这个。他迷路了，于是他问乌鸦，"你知道火车站在哪儿吗？"

"当然。"一只叫杰布的大乌鸦回答。"往左走，向右拐，一直走。"

"谢谢。"那个人微笑着说，匆匆离开。剩下的乌鸦（古怪，果酱，坏脾气，鸡蛋壳和麻子）把杰布围住。他们用乌鸦的语言交谈。

古怪说，"英语太难了！train station 是什么意思？"

杰布说，"我不知道。我只知道 '往左走，向右拐，一直走'。"

果酱说，"可是那个人很高兴！"

杰布说，"我只是学着把事情变简单。人们不喜欢复杂的回答。"

坏脾气说，"你太聪明了，杰布！"

杰布说，"我还知道了永远都要说 '当然'。人们不喜欢听到 '不'。"

鸡蛋壳说，"你的话对我们太有帮助了，杰布！"

杰布说，"是的，我知道。而且我反应很快。人们想要马上知道答案。不要说话太慢。"

麻子说，"你好聪明，杰布。我才知道。"

杰布说，"是的。我希望人们也会变聪明。那个人刚刚错过了这个角落的所有免费食品。"

寓意：　自负会导致错误。

Taking It a Step Further——Moral Prompts

*How would you change the ending of this fable, and what would a new moral be to this ending?

*People want quick answers, but why is this often a problem?

Fable 17 To Be King

The Lion was tired of his role as King of the Jungle. He decided to another animal to become King. The first two animals were the crane and the wolf. "So, what would you do if you were King of the Jungle?" asked the Lion to the crane.

The crane puffed up his feathers and said, "We need change Sire. Yes, change! First, Sire, I would order all of the frogs to the pond where we cranes can easily catch them. All bugs must also remain where we can see them. And, well, why not

have bats fly during the day like the birds?"

The Lion turned to the wolf: "How about you?"

"Sire, we need more rules! The jungle is out of control, Sire! Let's talk about those lying, cheating rabbits, moles, rats, and squirrels! My idea is to make some new rules. Rabbits can't run when they see a wolf. Moles can't hide. And rats and squirrels can't climb trees when a wolf chases them. You see, I want 'fair play.'"

The Lion closed his eyes and thought, and thought some more. Finally, he said, "Did I say 'King' of the Jungle? Oh, I am so sorry! I meant 'sing,' like 'Singer' of the Jungle. Uh, so, can you sing?" As neither could sing, both the wolf and the crane went home.

Moral: Power is rarely understood.

寓言 17　　要当国王

　　狮子厌倦了作为丛林之王的角色。他决定让别的动物来作国王。首先来的两个动物是仙鹤和狼。"如果你当了丛林之王，你会怎样做？"狮子问仙鹤。仙鹤竖起羽毛，说，"我们需要改变，陛下。是的，改变！我会命令所有的青蛙都到池塘里，我们仙鹤就可以轻松抓到他们。所有的虫子也必须停在我们能看到的地方。还有，为什么不让蝙蝠和其他的鸟一样，在白天飞行？"狮子又转向狼说，"你呢？"

　　"陛下，我们需要更多的规则！丛林已经失控，陛下！我们来说说那些说谎，骗人的兔子，鼹鼠，老鼠和松鼠！我的主意是制定一些新的规则。兔子看到狼，不能跑。鼹鼠不能躲起来。当狼追他们的时候，老鼠和松鼠不能爬到树上。你看，我想要公正的游戏。"

　　狮子闭上眼睛，想了想。最后，他说，"我说是丛林之王了吗？对不起，我的意思是'sing'（唱歌），就是丛林歌手。呃，你们会唱歌吗？"狼和仙鹤都不会唱歌，他们回家了。

寓意：　权力几乎不可理喻。

Taking It a Step Further——Moral Prompts

*Do you want a job or position in the future in which you have a lot of power?

*What are the common problems that the "powerful" have in life?

Fable 18 Endor

My dear frog friends, I have called you here because every day, the cranes eat us. The time has COME for us to EAT them. It's either EAT or be EATEN. RISE UP!"

Endor, the frog leader, looked over the cheering frogs, some- one asked a question. "How can we eat the cranes? We don't have teeth!"

Endor shouted back, "We don't NEED teeth to eat them. We will stomp them into mush!" The frogs agreed with very loud croaks. But a few frogs hopped away. Another frog asked a question. "How can we stomp them into mush when they are taller than us?"

"WHAT? WHAT? Are you so weak?" shouted back Endor. "Height is not important! WE are taller than the cranes when we sit on trees." Again, there were more croaks and more frogs hopped away.

As Endor suggested using cranes as amusement rides, cranes as transportation, and cranes as clowns and entertainment, a few more frogs hopped away. When Endor finished, he asked how many frogs would follow him. Only one frog, his mother, was still there.

Moral: Don't be surprised if others don't share your idealism.

寓言 18　　恩多

＂亲爱的青蛙朋友们，我把大家召集到这里，因为每天仙鹤吃我们。现在到时候我们该吃他们了。我们不去吃，就会被吃掉。让我们行动起来！＂

恩多，青蛙的领袖，看着兴奋的青蛙们。有人问了一个问题，＂我们怎么吃仙鹤？我们没有牙齿！＂

恩多大声喊，＂吃他们，我们不需要牙齿。我们把他们踩成肉泥！＂青蛙们大声鸣叫，表示赞同。可是有一些青蛙跳走了。另一只青蛙问了一个问题，＂他们比我们高大，我们怎么把他们踩成肉泥？＂

＂什么？什么？你们那么弱小吗？＂恩多大声说。＂高度不重要！我们坐在树上，就比仙鹤高。＂又有很多青蛙鸣叫着离开。

当恩多提议可以骑着仙鹤玩耍，用仙鹤作为交通工具，还可以把仙鹤当成小丑，更多的青蛙离开了。当恩多说完这些，只有一只青蛙愿意跟随他。他的妈妈仍然没有离开。

寓意：　用不着惊讶如果别人不同意你的想法。

Taking It a Step Further——Moral Prompts

*Are there any people today that you know who are like Endor?

*Are you an idealistic person?

Fable 19 A Sheep's Checklist

A lion fell in love with a sheep. He asked the sheep, "My dearest, what can I do? I want you to fall in love with me."

"Well," replied the sheep, "Here is my list of requirements."

1. Cut your hair. [ ]
2. Shave your face. [ ]
3. Remove your sharp claws and teeth. [ ]
4. Dye your hair white. [ ]
5. Perm your hair. [ ]
6. *Baaaaa* like a sheep. [ ]
7. Walk like a sheep. [ ]
8. Get some deodorant. [ ]
9. Use mouthwash. [ ]
10. Have nonviolent hobbies. [ ]

"Wait! Those are just the opposite of my requirements!" replied the lion. The lion started to walk away. Then he called back, "I should find a lion, and you should find another sheep."

Moral: Love doesn't ask for change.

寓言 19　　羊的清单

　　狮子爱上了羊。他问羊，＂亲爱的，我该怎么办呢？我想让你爱上我。＂

　　＂好啊。＂羊回答说，＂这是我的需求列表。＂

1. 把头发剪掉。　　　　　　　　　　[ ]
2. 刮脸。　　　　　　　　　　　　　[ ]
3. 除掉锋利的爪子和牙齿。　　　　　[ ]
4. 把头发染白。　　　　　　　　　　[ ]
5. 烫头。　　　　　　　　　　　　　[ ]
6. 像羊一样咩咩叫。　　　　　　　　[ ]
7. 像羊一样走路。　　　　　　　　　[ ]
8. 找到一个除臭剂。　　　　　　　　[ ]
9. 用漱口水。　　　　　　　　　　　[ ]
10. 不许暴力。　　　　　　　　　　　[ ]

　　＂等等！那些都是和我的需求相反的啊！＂狮子回答。狮子走开了。他给羊回电话说，＂我应该找一只狮子，你应该找一只羊。＂

　　寓意：　爱一个人不会要求他改变。

Taking It a Step Further——Moral Prompts

*Some say that everyone has a checklist when looking for a romantic partner? Is this true with you?

*What is another good moral for this fable?

*If a future boy/girlfriend asked you to change something about your appearance or behavior, would you do it?

Fable 20 The Snake and the Rat

"Let's make peace! We, snakes and you rats have always been at war. Why?" asked the snake to a rat named Rufus. "Come on in my snake hole, and we will drink to a new time of peace," the snake added.

Rufus was surprised, but cautiously replied, "Yes, but the fox says you snakes can not be trusted!"

The snake hissed, "You just don't understand me. If you come now, I will give you a snake charm because you are my friend."

"A snake charm? But, wait, the birds say that steal everything. Snakes are all thieves."

"Ah, that is a . . . cultural problem. It's a simple clash of values. Now, let's not keep 'peace' waiting. If you hurry, I will have time to make some bread."

"Stop! The moles told me that snakes are poisonous. All that your food is poison!"

"That, my friend, is jealousy. Moles are grumpy, and they're always alone. Now, come, come! If you hurry, I am sure I can give you some money, too!"

"Money? Well, why didn't you say that?" replied the rat. The rat then jumped into the snake hole. And the snake quickly ate him.

Moral: Peace is not in one's words but in one's heart.

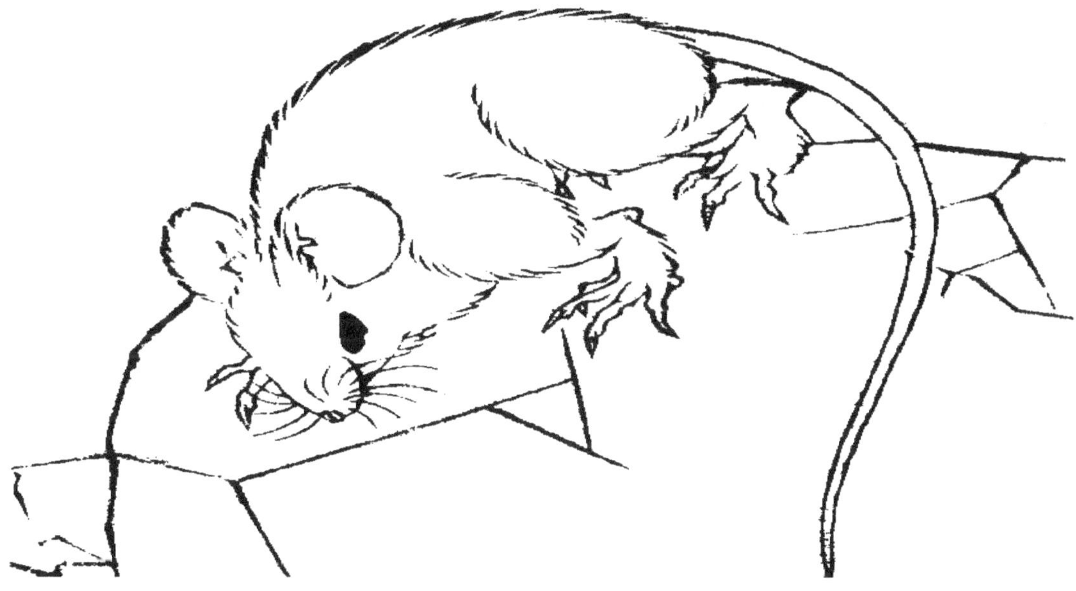

寓言 20　蛇和老鼠

〝我们和好吧。我们蛇和你们老鼠一直都在敌对。为什么？〞蛇问一只叫卢夫斯的老鼠。〝到我的蛇洞里来。让我们为了和平的新时代，喝一杯。〞蛇补充说。卢夫斯很惊讶，但是小心地回答，〝好的。可是狐狸说你们蛇是不能信赖的。〞

蛇发出嘶嘶声，〝你不明白我的意思。如果你现在来，我给你一个蛇的小饰物，因为你是我的朋友。〞

〝蛇的饰物？可是，等等，鸟说你们偷所有的东西。蛇都是小偷。〞

〝啊，那是。。。那是一个文化问题。是价值观的冲突。现在，让我们保持和平。如果你着急的话，我有时间可以做些面包。〞

〝等等！鼹鼠告诉我蛇都是有毒的。所有你们的食物都是毒药！〞

〝那个，我的朋友，就是嫉妒！鼹鼠喜欢抱怨，他们都是独来独往。现在来吧。来呀。如果你着急，我保证还会给你一些钱。〞

〝钱？好吧。你刚才为什么不说？〞老鼠回答。老鼠于是跳到了蛇洞里。蛇马上就把他吃了。

寓意：　和平不在一个人的甜言蜜语，而在心里。

Taking It a Step Further——Moral Prompts

*Can money and wealth ever buy friendship and peace?

*Who is the most "peaceful" person that you know?

Fable 21　The Careful Donkey

Each night a wolf that came. So a donkey climbed up on its owner's roof. The donkey knew he was safe now. He laughed and laughed. Then he slipped on some tile and fell over the edge of the house.

On the ground and in great pain, the donkey said to him- self, "That roof is as dangerous as the wolf! I better think a long time about what makes me safe!"

Moral: Think twice about what can make you safe.

寓言 21　　谨慎的驴

每天晚上狼都会来。所以驴就爬上主人的房顶。他知道这样他才安全。他开心大笑。于是他滑倒在了一些瓦片上，坠落出了房顶的边缘。

驴在地上，痛苦地对自己说，〝那个房顶和狼一样危险！我最好花时间想想自己怎样才安全！〞

寓意：　要反复思考怎样才是安全。

Taking It a Step Further——Moral Prompts

*The fable cautions you to think twice about the choices you make: do you do this?

*What are you careful about?

Fable 22 The Last Time

A teacher saw a snake slowly eat a rat. He talked about the cruelty of animals. "You see! Humans are so much better than snakes. Look at this cruelty. The snake is so bad!" The teacher told his students, "We must stop this evil now." Then the teacher and his students gave the snake a beating.

The snake crawled back to his hole and family. He told his family, "THAT is the LAST time I will ever help people. Those rats can destroy their fields and eat all their corn. I don't care!"

Moral: Violence always has a consequence.

寓言 22　　最后一次

　　一个老师看到蛇在慢慢吃一只老鼠。他开始讲述动物的残酷。〝你们看！人类比蛇好多了。看看这多残酷。蛇太坏了！〞

　　老师对学生说，〝我们现在必须制止残酷。〞

　　于是老师和学生们把蛇揍了一顿。蛇爬回蛇洞，找到他的家人。他对家人说，〝那是最后一次我帮助人类。那些老鼠毁坏他们的田地，吃他们的玉米。我不会在意了！

寓意： 暴力总会有恶果。

Taking It a Step Further——Moral Prompts

　　*Do you really think that violence has a consequence?

　　*What is another good moral to this fable?

Volume 2

Fable 1　The Cat and the Bell

Some rats tried to put a bell on a cat for many years. They could never do it. "We should move to the forest. It is better to die there of starvation than to stay here. The cat will eat us," said one rat.

"That cat is an eating machine," complained another rat. "It is always hungry. It eats anything that it sees," added an- other rat.

"How about raising the bell over the cat?" suggested one young rat. "When it sleeps, we can lower the bell. Then we can tie it on the cat."

"We tried that last year, and the cat ate two rats," said an older rat. The rats talked about more plans. Finally one small rat said, "Let's push the mousetrap out into the kitchen. This cat likes to eat everything. Maybe it will eat the cheese in the mouse- trap. When it is trapped, we will put the bell on it."

The rats all agreed. They pushed the mousetrap out. And they were very surprised! The cat tried to get the cheese. It couldn't get out of the trap. A hundred rats jumped on it and tied the bell tightly around its neck. Then the rats were safe and free.

Moral: Greedy ones are easy to trap.

寓言 1　猫和铃铛

已经有很多年，一些老鼠试图在猫身上挂一个铃铛。他们永远也做不到。

"我们应该搬到森林里。在那里饿死也比在这儿呆着好。猫会吃掉我们的。"一只老鼠说。

"那只猫就是一台吃东西的机器。"另一只老鼠抱怨道。"它总是很饿。它吃掉它看到的任何东西。"另一只老鼠补充道。

"把铃铛缠绕到猫身上怎么样？"一只小老鼠建议。"当它睡觉的时候，我们可以把铃铛放到低处。然后把它绑在猫身上。"

"我们去年尝试过。那只猫吃了两只老鼠。"一只大老鼠说。老鼠们讨论了更多的计划。最后，一只小老鼠说："我们还是把捕鼠器推进厨房吧。那只猫喜欢吃所有的东西。也许它会把捕鼠器里的奶酪吃掉。当它被夹住的时候，我们可以把铃铛系好。"

老鼠们都同意这个想法。他们把捕鼠器推出去，然后非常吃惊地看到猫试图吃到奶酪，它无法摆脱捕鼠器。一百只老鼠跳到猫身上，将铃铛紧紧地绑在它的脖子上。于是老鼠们又安全又自由。

寓意：贪婪的人容易被困住。

Taking It a Step Further——Moral Prompts

* Have you ever seen any greedy people in your life?
* What is another good moral for his fables?

Fable 2   The Swan, Crow, and the Alligator

A very hungry alligator saw a crow and a swan on the side of a lake. He called out to them. "You two are so beautiful! I've never seen such beauty!" The crow was quiet. But the swan said, "I'm so happy! You can see how beautiful I am!"

The alligator replied, "It's your beauty and your charm. Come closer so that we can talk." The crow flew up into a tree. But the swan quickly jumped into the water. And the alligator ate the swan.

Moral: Flattery only works with the vain.

寓言 2   天鹅，乌鸦和鳄鱼

一只饥饿的鳄鱼在湖边看见了一只乌鸦和一只天鹅。他向他们呼喊，"你们两个是如此美丽！我从来没见过有人这么漂亮的！"乌鸦很安静。天鹅却说："我很高兴！你看我有多美丽！"

鳄鱼回答说："这是你的美丽和魅力。靠近我一点，我们可以谈谈。"乌鸦飞到了树上。可是天鹅却马上跳到了水里。于是，鳄鱼吃掉了天鹅。

寓意：　自负的人才会相信奉承。

Taking It a Step Further——Moral Prompts

* Do you think beauty makes one happy?
* Do you know of someone who is vain?

Fable 3   The Goat and the Tiger

A small goat was standing on the roof of his owner's house. He saw a tiger passing by. The goat began to tease the tiger. "You are so slow! And you are so ugly! No one likes you!"

The tiger looked up and replied, "I hear you. I hear you. And I promise you something. One day you will have to come down from that roof. On that day, you will have something to fear."

Moral: Sooner or later you will have to face the consequences of what you have said.

寓言 3　　山羊和老虎

一只小山羊站在主人家的屋顶上。他看到一只老虎经过。山羊开始取笑老虎。"你走得太慢了！而且那么丑！没有人喜欢你！"

老虎抬起头，回答说："我听到了。我听到了。我向你保证。有一天，你将不得不从那个屋顶上下来。那一天，你会感到恐惧。"

寓意：　早晚我们都要为自己说的话负责。

Taking It a Step Further——Moral Prompts

* Do bad words affect you negatively?

* Have you seen someone insult another person lately? How did you react?

Fable 4　　The Two Pots

Once there were two pots. One pot was made of clay. The other pot was made of metal. Their owner was throwing them away. The clay pot said to the metal pot, "It's all your fault. You are ugly and you are rusty. That's why our owner is throwing us away. You are careless. Now I have to pay for it!"

The metal pot replied, "What? Our owner is throwing us out because you leak. And your paint is peeling off. It's all your fault!" The owner heard the pots arguing and said, "Your arguing is just showing me again that it is time for a pot that doesn't cause me problems."

Moral: Arguing produces more problems than answers .

寓言4　两个罐子

从前有两个罐子。一个是用黏土制成的。另一个是金属。主人把它们扔掉了。粘土罐子对金属罐子说："都是你的错。你长得丑，还生锈了。这就是为什么主人把我们扔掉。你不够小心，现在我需要为此付出代价！"

金属罐子回答说："你说什么？主人把我们扔掉是因为你漏水，而且外部的涂层已经剥落。都是你的错！"店主听到他们的争吵，说："你们的争吵再次让我确信，是时候换新的罐子了，这样才不会给我带来麻烦。"

寓意：争论会带来更多问题而不是答案。

Taking It a Step Further——Moral Prompts

* What kinds of things cause you to argue?

* In arguments, are there actually winners and losers, or does everyone just lose?

Fable 5　The Fir-Tree and the Thorn Bush

A fir tree was teasing a thorn bush. "You are so ugly and useless. It must be hard!" The thorn bush replied, "Yes. I'm ugly and I'm useless. But people stay away from me. You are not ugly, so children play in your branches and break them. You are not useless, so their parents chop you down for firewood." The fir tree replied, "Yes, but at least they will keep me around. It will be just a matter of time before they take some shovels and take you away to the dump."

Moral: The useless will sooner or later be thrown away.

寓言 5　　杉树和荆棘丛

　　一棵杉树戏弄荆棘丛。"你长相丑陋，又没有用。对你来说太难了！"荆棘丛回答说："是的。我很丑，也没有用。但是人们远离我。你长得不丑，所以孩子们在树枝上玩耍，还折断它们。你有用途啊，所以他们的父母把你砍成柴火。"杉树回答说："是的，但是至少他们会保留我在周围。他们迟早会拿铁锹把你挖走，送到垃圾场。"

寓意：没用的东西迟早会被替换。

* Are there some useless things in your life that actually shouldn't be thrown away?

* What kinds of things do you usually throw away?

Fable 6   The Bat and The Rat

One day a bat fell to the ground. He met a rat that was searching for food in the garbage. The rat was puzzled. What kind of animal was this? He said, "Oh my. You are the strangest rat I have ever seen."

The bat was afraid. He thought the rat might attack him because he wasn't a rat. He replied, "Well, I come from a family of . . . country rats. We live far, far away. That is why we look funny." The rat's eyes narrowed and it began to sniff. "You also smell real funny too."

The bat was desperately trying to get its wings in order. He answered, "Well, that is our… our. . . perfume. Yes, we take a bath in special water so we can smell this way." The rat was even more suspicious now.

He pointed to the bat's wings. He asked, "Well, what are those things on your back? I've never seen anything like them.

"Uh, oh these things? Well, they are an extra covering to keep us warm. It's so cold in the countryside at night." The rat looked at the bat's wings some more. Finally, he stepped back and said, "Hmm . . . OK then. If you say that you are a rat, then you are a rat. Come over here and get busy. Help me to sort through this garbage. If we are lucky, we will be finished by morning!"

Moral: Don't be afraid to show how you are different.

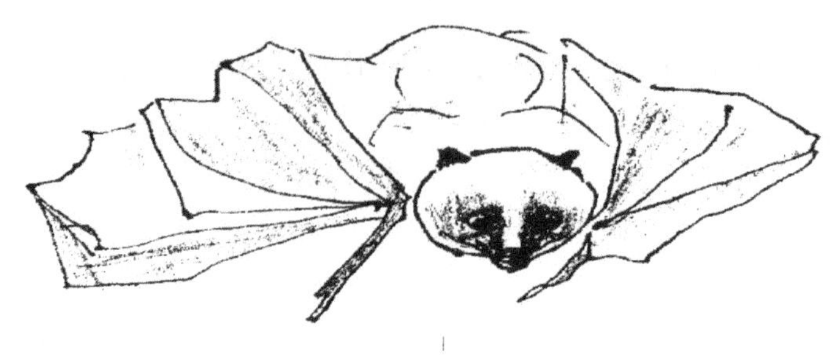

寓言6　　蝙蝠和老鼠

一天，一只蝙蝠掉到了地上。他遇到了一只老鼠，正在垃圾里寻找食物。老鼠很迷惑，这是什么动物呢？他说："天哪，你是我见过的最奇怪的老鼠。"

蝙蝠很害怕。他认为老鼠可能会攻击他，因为他不是老鼠的同类。他回答说："嗯，我来自一个。。。郊外老鼠的家庭。我们生活在很远，很远的地方。所以我们看起来很可笑。"老鼠眯起眼睛，开始用鼻子闻，"你身上的味道也很奇怪。"

蝙蝠绝望地试图把翅膀梳理整齐。他回答说："那是。。。那是我们的。。。香水。是的，我们在特殊的水里洗澡，所以我们可以闻起来这样的味道。"那只老鼠变得更加怀疑。

他指着蝙蝠的翅膀，问道："好，你背上那些东西是什么？我从没见过它们。"

"哦，这些东西？嗯，它们是让我们保暖的遮盖物。乡下的晚上特别冷。"老鼠又看了看蝙蝠的翅膀。最后，他退后一步说："嗯。。。那好吧。如果你说你是一只老鼠，那你就是一只老鼠。过来这里帮忙吧。帮我整理一下这些垃圾。如果幸运的话，我们早上之前就能完成！"

寓意：　不要害怕展示自己的不同。

Taking It a Step Further——Moral Prompts

* Do you try to blend in with your friends a lot?

* How are you different from your friends and parents

Fable 7　The Boy Hunting Locusts

A boy was hunting for some locusts. He saw a scorpion. He did not know what kind of bug it was, so he reached down to catch it. The scorpion backed up and showed its stinger. Then it yelled, "If you try to catch me, you will really lose your interest in collecting bugs. Trust me!"

Moral: Painful experiences can change your interests.

寓言　7　　　抓蚂蚱的男孩儿

一个男孩正在抓蚂蚱。他看到一只蝎子。他不知道那是什么虫子，所以伸手去抓。蝎子后退，露出了它的毒刺。然后大声说：“如果你想抓住我，你肯定会对收集昆虫丧失兴趣。相信我！”

寓意：　痛苦的经历会改变一个人的兴趣。

Taking It a Step Further——Moral Prompts

*What was your last painful experience, and what did it teach you?

*Are you more afraid of insects than of animals? What kind makes you afraid the most?

Fable 8   The Two Snakes

Two very old snakes met under a bush. They had been friends a long time ago. "Alfred," called out one. "Is it really you? It's been such a long time. My goodness, you don't have any teeth."

"Henry, it's been too long! We're both so very old now. And I see that you are as blind as a bat!"

"Ah, I'm a little blind. But I can see that I am still a little stronger than you, my good friend," replied Alfred.

This soon led to some arguing, and then to a challenge. The two snakes began to wrestle. The noise caught the attention of two snake hunters. They caught the snakes for their snake show at school.

Moral: Showing off always gets attention.

寓言 8　　两条蛇

两条年龄很大的蛇在灌木丛下相遇。他们很久以前就是朋友。"阿尔弗雷德，"一条蛇大声喊道。"真的是你吗？已经好久了没见了。天哪，你没有牙齿了。"

"亨利，实在是太久了！我们俩现在都这么老了。我觉得你像蝙蝠一样眼盲！"

"啊，我有点眼瞎了。但我感到我还是比你强壮一些，我的好朋友。"阿尔弗雷德说。

这很快导致了一场争论，接着就是挑战。两条蛇开始搏斗。喧闹声引起了两个猎蛇者的注意。他们抓到了蛇，用作在学校的表演。

寓意：　炫耀会引人注意。

Taking It a Step Further——Moral Prompts

* What is another good moral for this fable?

* How would you show off to get attention?

Fable 9   The Man Bitten by a Dog

A man saw his friend walking a very big, very ugly dog. The friend called out and wanted to chat, but the man stayed far away.

He was afraid the dog would bite him. After a short chat, the man walked on. He soon saw another friend with a pretty little poodle.

He greeted his friend and said, "What a cute dog you have. What's its name?" The man reached down to pet the dog, but the dog jumped up and bit him on the hand.

Moral: The small and pretty can be as dangerous as the large and ugly.

寓言 9　　被狗咬的人

一个人看到他的朋友正在遛一只很大，很丑的狗。朋友大声喊，想和他聊天，可是这个人远远地躲开。

他担心狗会咬他。于是短暂地交谈之后，这个人继续往前走。很快他看到另一个朋友带着一只贵宾犬。

他向这个朋友打招呼说："真是一只可爱的狗。它叫什么名字？"这个人弯腰伸手去抚摸小狗，结果小狗跳起来，咬住他的手。

寓意：外表娇小漂亮，也可能和巨大丑陋的东西一样充满危险。

Taking It a Step Further——Moral Prompts

* What are some small but dangerous animals?

* How do you think people view you? Are you approachable? Do you look dangerous or unfriendly?

Fable 10   The Fruit Trees

A group of fruit trees was discussing which of them had the tastiest fruit.

The Orange Tree: "My fruit must be the tastiest. Man makes juice out of it and drinks it every day."

The Apple Tree: "So what? He makes juice out of my fruit, too, and also makes pies and pastry."

The Pear Tree: "Pies?! So what? Man takes my fruit and puts it in cans. And my fruit gets the best price, too. The most expensive fruit must be the tastiest." The argument got so loud that Mother Nature came. Because they were quarreling so much, she gave each tree its own harvest season.

Moral: Quarreling usually makes others solve the problem.

寓言 10　　果树

果树们在讨论到底谁结的果子最美味。

橘子树："我的果实一定是最好吃的。人们用它做果汁，每天都喝。"

苹果树："那又怎么样？他们也用我的果实榨汁，而且做成馅饼和糕点。"

梨树："馅饼？！那有什么？人们把我的果实放到罐头里。我的果实价格也最高。最贵的水果一定是最美味的。"争论如此激烈，以至于大自然母亲都来了。由于他们争吵得太多，她给予每棵果树属于自己的收获季节。

寓意：争吵通常需要别人来解决问题。

Taking It a Step Further——Moral Prompts

* Who usually ends up solving your quarrels?

* Do men quarrel more than women or do women have more disputes?

Fable 11　The Mother and The Wine Jar

A mother, in her old age, found an empty wine jar behind her son's house. It had been full of very good wine. The fragrance was still in the jar. As she smelled the jar, she said, "Oh, how delicious this wine must have been. I can still smell the joy and laughter in its fragrance."

Sniffing it some more, the mother frowned. Then she thought, "Why didn't my son invite me to have some of the wine?"

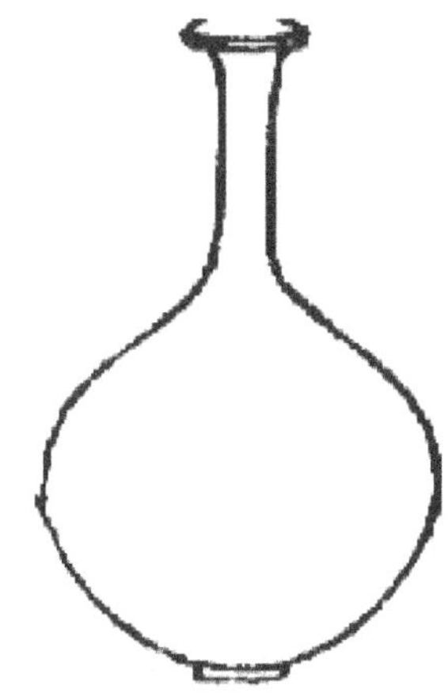

Moral: Happiness comes from sharing.

寓言 11　　母亲和葡萄酒罐

　　一位年老的母亲在儿子家的后院发现了一个空的葡萄酒罐。罐子用来盛上等的葡萄酒，香味还留在里面。

　　当她闻到罐子的味道时，她说："哦，这酒一定是非常美味。我依然可以感受到芳香中的欢乐和笑声。"

　　母亲又闻了闻，皱起了眉头。随后，她想："为什么我儿子没有邀请我来喝酒？"

寓意：幸福来自于分享。

Taking It a Step Further——Moral Prompts

* They say that the person who has the most "toys" wins in life! Do you agree?

* How often do you share your things? What things would you never share?

Fable 12 The Pig, the Sheep, and the Goat

A fat pig, a sheep, and a goat were tied up in a pen. The sheep and goat looked at the pig and saw that every day the pig was well fed. Yet it did nothing in return. The sheep and the goat began to question the pig.

"You lazy good-for-nothing," said the sheep. "I have to be shaved every month. I lose all of my wool. What do you do? Nothing!"

The goat complained, "I have to give the farmer all my milk every day. All you do is to sleep and eat. So, what's the secret, huh?"

"It's the way I smell," the pig answered. "The farmer likes it."

"But you smell horrible, like last week's garbage," protested the goat.

"And don't forget that I eat last week's garbage, too," added the pig. "The farmer also likes the way I look. He never cleans me."

"But how can that be?!" protested the sheep. "You're disgusting!

"If that's the way to have an easy life, let's do it, too," said the goat to the sheep. The sheep and the goat started lying around in the mud. They tried to look and smell as bad as they could. Finally, the farmer came to the pen. He looked at the pig, and said to his friend, "OK. I think the pig is fat enough to take to market. It should make some good sausages."

Then he looked at the other two dirty animals and added, "Take these two disgusting creatures, too. I don't want to have such dirty animals on my farm."

Moral: The "easy way" in life has a price.

寓言 12　　猪，绵羊和山羊

一只肥猪，一只绵羊和一只山羊被绑在围栏上。绵羊和山羊看着猪每天被喂得饱饱。可是它却不需要做任何事情。绵羊和山羊开始向猪咨询。

"你这个懒家伙，"绵羊说，"我每个月都要被剃光。我失去了所有的羊毛。你做什么了？什么都没做！"

山羊抱怨说："我每天必须把牛奶全部提供给农夫。你却只会睡觉和吃饭。到底是怎么回事呢？"

"这因为我的气味。"猪回答，"农夫喜欢。"

"可是你闻起来糟透了，像上个星期的垃圾。"山羊抗议说。

"别忘了我也吃前一周的垃圾。"猪补充说。"农夫还喜欢我的样子。他从不让我洗澡。"

"但是那怎么可能？！"绵羊抗议说。"你那么令人恶心！

"如果那样，可以过轻松的生活，让我们也尝试一下吧。"山羊对绵羊说。

绵羊和山羊开始躺在烂泥中。他们试图尽可能地看起来丑陋，闻起来糟糕。最后，农夫来到了围栏。他看着那头猪，对他的朋友说："好了。我觉得这头猪足够肥，可以送到市场。它应该可以做成一些好香肠。"

然后他看着另外两只肮脏的动物，补充说："也把这两个令人恶心的畜生带走。我不想我的农场里有这么肮脏的动物。"

寓意：生活中的"简便方法"要付出代价。

Taking It a Step Further——Moral Prompts

* Do you know of anyone who usually tries to "cut corners" and make a task easier for him or herself?

* Do people really know if you didn't do something completely "perfect"?

Fable 13   The Fisherman and The Seagull

"How beautiful it looks," said a young seagull to his mother. They were watching a man tossing a huge net into the sea. "It must be his hobby."

His mother replied, "My son, it's a mystery. Don't bother him."

The young seagull was puzzled. He watched for a few minutes, then he said, "Mother, I must go and ask him what he is doing."

As the young seagull flew over the man, he didn't see the other nets that the men were throwing. The seagull got caught in another net.

Moral: Curiosity is the worst net of all.

寓言 13　　渔夫和海鸥

"它真漂亮。"一只小海鸥对他的母亲说。他们看着一个人把巨大的网扔进海里。"这一定是他的爱好。"

他的母亲回答说："我的儿子，这是一个谜。不要打扰他。"

小海鸥感到困惑。他看了一会儿，然后说："妈妈，我必须去问问他在干什么。"

当小海鸥飞过那个人的头顶，它没有注意到男人扔出的又一张网。海鸥被罩住了。

寓意：　好奇心是最糟糕的网。

Taking It a Step Further——Moral Prompts

* What kinds of things are you curious about?

* Have you ever asked too many questions that irritated people?

Fable 14   The Inn

Two hungry brothers, Mandal and Jemel, stopped in an inn for a meal. They both ordered a bowl of oat- meal. They quickly ate and enjoyed the food. Then the cook said, "Well, if you liked that, you should love my bread, chicken, and wine." Mandal said that he didn't need to eat any more, but Jemel eagerly ordered more food.   As Jemel buttered his bread and drank his wine, he said to his brother, "Mmmm . . . it's really delicious, brother. Come on. Have some."

"No thanks. I don't really want any," replied Mandal.

"How could you NOT want this?" asked Jemel. "This food is really DELICIOUS." During the evening, Jemel ordered and ate smoked salmon, pot roast, sweet peas, okra, and lemon pudding.

Mandal said, "No" to everything. Finally, the cook came again. She said, "Well, if you liked all of that, you will LOVE my dessert—strawberry cake. It's famous throughout the land."

"I KNOW, I KNOW," said Mandal. "I will have two pieces! I waited for it." Jemel, however, was too sick. He wanted to eat some delicious cake, but he just couldn't eat even one bite.

Moral: Moderation tastes better than too much.

寓言 14　　旅店

曼达尔（Mandal）和杰梅尔（Jemel）这两个饥饿的弟兄在一家旅馆吃饭。他们都点了一碗燕麦饭，很快地吃，非常享受。然后厨师说："不错。如果你们喜欢燕麦饭的话，也应该喜欢我做的面包，鸡肉和葡萄酒。"曼达尔说不需要再吃了，但杰梅尔急切地点了更多的食物。

杰梅尔给面包涂着黄油，喝着酒，对哥哥说："嗯。。。真地很好吃。兄弟，来一些尝尝吧。"

"不用了，谢谢。我真地不想吃。"曼达尔回答。

"你为什么不想要？"杰梅尔问。"这些食物的确美味。"晚上，杰梅尔点了烟熏鲑鱼，烤肉，甜豌豆，秋葵和柠檬布丁。

曼达尔对所有食物说"不"。终于，厨师又来了。她说："不错。如果你们喜欢这些食物，那么您会爱上我做的甜点-草莓蛋糕。它在整个国家都很有名。"

"我知道，我知道，"曼达尔说。"我要两块！我很期待。"但是，杰梅尔（Jemel）太不舒服了。他想吃美味的蛋糕，可是连一口都吃不下。

寓意： 有节制比吃得多美味。

Taking It a Step Further——Moral Prompts

* Have you eaten too much recently?

* Is it really true: does the second piece of pie taste less tasty than the first?

Fable 15　The Tunnel

The weather was very, very cold. A young snake decided to make a tunnel to sleep in. However, the loose sand kept caving in on her. After an hour, a mole passed by. The snake asked the mole for help.

"Ah," said the mole. "You need to put rocks around the sides of your tunnel." And he hurried away. The snake pushed many rocks in and around the sides of her tunnel, but the sand was still falling down on her. A rabbit's advice was no help, either. And a badger's suggestion to "give up!" was useless.

As it got colder, a hedgehog scampered by. The snake begged the hedgehog, "Oh, help me, Mr. Hedgehog. I need to build a tunnel because it's so cold."

"Oh sure," the hedgehog replied. For the next hour, the hedgehog scooped out the earth and showed the snake exactly how to do it. The snake learned that tunnels are built not with words, but with deeds.

Moral: Those who advise and those who help are rarely the same people.

寓言 15　　地洞

天气非常非常冷。一条小蛇决定挖一条地洞睡觉。可是，松散的沙子不断坍塌下来。一小时后，一只鼹鼠经过。蛇向鼹鼠求助。

"啊，"鼹鼠说。"你需要在地洞的周边放些石头。"然后他就匆匆走了。蛇把很多石头推进地洞，放在地洞的周边。但是仍然有沙子落在她身上。兔子的建议也没有用。獾直接建议它放弃。

随着天气变冷，一只刺猬蹦蹦跳跳地经过。蛇恳求刺猬，"哦，刺猬先生，请帮帮我。我需要建造一个地洞，因为太冷了。"

"哦，当然。"刺猬回答说。接下来的一个小时，刺猬挖出了很多土，向蛇展示该如何做。蛇明白了，地洞不是用文字搭建的，而是用行为。

寓意：提出建议的人通常不提供帮助。

Taking It a Step Further——Moral Prompts

* Do people ever listen to your advice?
* Do help people a lot?

Fable 16   A New Anthill

A group of ants was working very hard. They were trying to carry a huge corn cob. They decided to rest in the summer sun. It wasn't long before the ants started discussing their very hard lives.

Vox, the group leader, said, "I just wish I could take a vacation." Zok, a carrier, mentioned that three good dinners and several milk shakes would be better. "Hurrah!" cheered the rest of the ants. A very tired carrier, named Wod, finally spoke up. "You know, I think we ALL need to go and rest by the lake."

Everyone said, "Yes!!!" to Wod's idea. So, the ants all marched to the lake. Later, Wod suggested that they get some nice grass to lie on, to eat the corn they had, and to make their own camp. The ants said "Great idea!" to all Wod's suggestions.

Then Wod thought of new rules: "Eat as much as you want," "relax by the lake for two hours a day," and "work only when you want to work."

All the ants agreed with hurrahs every time. Soon, Wod's dream of his own anthill came true.

Moral: Big changes are best disguised as lots of small, safe ideas.

寓言 16　　新蚁丘

一群蚂蚁在努力工作。他们试图搬运一个巨大的玉米芯。他们决定在烈日下休息一会儿。很快，蚂蚁们开始讨论他们的艰辛生活。

小组组长沃克斯（Vox）说："我只是希望我可以有一个假期。"搬运工佐克（Zok）说，要是有三顿丰盛的晚餐和几杯奶昔就更好了。"哇！"

其余的蚂蚁欢呼起来。一位名叫沃德（Wod）的搬运工非常疲惫。它终于开口说，"你们知道，我觉得我们都需要在湖边休息。"

"是的！！！"大家都赞成沃德的想法。于是所有的蚂蚁都向湖边进发。后来，沃德建议他们准备些松软的草，可以躺在上面。还可以吃玉米，并且自己搭建帐篷。"好主意！"蚂蚁们都赞成沃德的建议。

随后，沃德想到了新的规则："想吃多少，就吃多少"，"每天在湖边放松两小时"和"只有在想工作时才工作"。

所有的蚂蚁每次都高声欢呼，表示赞同。不久，沃德实现了自己的蚁丘梦。

寓意：大的改变最好从很多细小，安全的想法开始。

Taking It a Step Further——Moral Prompts

* What kinds of small changes should you make in your life?
* Do you like big changes in your routine, and school life?

Fable 17　The Errand

A mother told her son, Garry, to take some money to his grandmother. "Grandmother needs the money, so don't stop anywhere on the way. And no beer!" she said.

As Garry walked into town, he saw a pub. The pub owner waved to Garry and brought him inside. Garry told the owner his mother's rule about beer, but the pub owner said, "My BOY, we have too many rules. Rules are like the bars of a cage, and you need some 'liquid' to squeeze through the bars and get out of the cage. Have some fun."

So, Garry sat down and had a beer. An old man showed him how to play a game of dice. The old man said, "I know you are poor, so we will use my own money." Garry soon won most of the man's money. The second hour, the man suggested, "Garry, let's start using your money to play. It's only fair.

Garry agreed. He was winning, he saw no problem. But the old man won back his own money and all of Garry's money.

Garry felt his empty pockets and cried, "Oh please, PLEASE, sir. I REALLY need to give that money to my grandmother. She needs it."

"Your grandmother needs the money? That is what ALL the boys say when they lose. Garry started to complain and the man laughed, "I know, Garry. Your grandmother sent me to follow you and to teach you lesson about gambling." Garry could only say, "Oh - and WHAT a lesson!"

Moral: Temptation is a teacher.

寓言 17　　差事

一位母亲告诉她的儿子加里（Garry）给祖母送些钱。"祖母需要这些钱，所以不要在途中停留。而且不要喝啤酒！"她说。

当加里走进城里，他看到了一家酒吧。店主向加里挥手，将他带入房中。加里告诉了店主他母亲有关啤酒的规定，但是店主说："我的孩子，我们有太多规定。规则就像笼子的栏杆一样，你需要一些"液体"一样的东西，才能挤过栏杆，离开笼子。玩得开心。"

于是，加里坐下来喝了啤酒。一位老人向他展示如何玩骰子游戏。老人说："我知道你很穷，所以我们用我自己的钱来玩。"加里很快就赢得了老人的大部分钱。接下来的一小时，那个男人建议，"加里，让我们用你的钱玩吧。这是为了公平。"

加里同意了。他在赢钱，没觉得有问题。可是老人赢回了他自己的钱和加里的全部的钱。

加里摸着自己的空口袋，大喊："哦，拜托，先生。我真地需要把钱交给我的祖母。她需要钱。"

"你的祖母需要钱吗？那是所有男孩在输钱时说的话。"加里开始抱怨，那个男人笑了，"我知道，加里。你的祖母让我跟随你，并且教会你有关赌博的事情。"加里只能说："哦，这是一个教训！"

寓意：诱惑是一位老师。

Taking It a Step Further——Moral Prompts

* What tempts you the most?
* What is another moral for this fable?

Fable 18   Say What?

One day, a rich man died. His son's family inherited his large mansion. During the first few months, the mother asked the father to wash the windows.

The husband replied, "Look! They're OK. They look clean enough. We shouldn't clean too much. It would just make the place look too nice. The neighbors would be jealous" The father returned to his computer game.

During the next year, the steps began to crack, and a group of rats moved into the house. Again, the mother asked the father to fix the steps and kill the rats.

The father looked up from his TV program and replied, "Look. We just have to learn to step over the small cracks. And the rats have a right to live here, too." During the next two years, the roof began to leak, some windows were broken, mold began to grow along the pipes, weeds began to grow in the lawn, and some pipes began leaking. The father made some small efforts to correct these problems. Then he went back to his poker game.

One Saturday, the family went to the beach. Some robbers saw the house, thought that it was empty, and robbed it. An hour later, a city official drove by, saw the mess, and decided the house needed to be torn down.

Moral: Neglect opens the doors to all of the wrong people.

寓言 18   你说什么？

一天，一个有钱人死了。他儿子的家人继承了他的豪宅。在最初的几个月中，妻子要求丈夫洗窗户。

丈夫回答说："看啊！他们没问题，很干净。我们不用做太多清扫。那只会使这个地方看起来太漂亮。邻居们会嫉妒地。"丈夫接着玩电脑游戏。

第二年，台阶开始破裂，一群老鼠搬进了房子。再次，妻子要求丈夫修理台阶，并除掉老鼠。

丈夫看着电视节目，抬起头回答说："看呐。我们只需要学习如何迈过这个小裂缝。老鼠们也有权力住在这里。"在接下来的两年中，屋顶开始漏水，窗户也碎了，霉菌开始沿着管道蔓延，杂草在草坪生长，一些管道也开始漏水。丈夫做了些小小的努力，进行了维修。然后他又去玩扑克游戏。

一个周六，一家人去了海滩。一些强盗看到这个房子，以为房子没有人住，随后开始抢劫。一个小时后，一位市政官员开车驶过，看到了破败的景象，决定将这所房子拆掉。

寓意：疏忽向所有恶人敞开大门。

Taking It a Step Further——Moral Prompts

*What kinds of things or chores do you often neglect?

*In looking around your city, what areas do you think are "neglected"?

Fable 19 The Dieting Fish

A fish pond owner fed his fish every day. For two months, he praised his fish when they became fat, long, and beautiful. This gave him a higher price at the market. One hot day, he noticed that one fish was not eating.

He asked the fish, "Why do you not eat like your brothers and sisters?" The fish answered, "Oh, I see that the more my brothers and sisters eat, the more they disappear."

Moral: Learn from the "success" of others.

寓言 19　　减肥的鱼

鱼塘的主人每天都喂鱼。有两个月，当鱼变得肥美，变大，变得美丽时，他称赞了他的鱼。这些鱼卖出了更高的市场价格。炎热的一天，他注意到一条鱼没有进食。

他问那条鱼，"你为什么不像你的兄弟姐妹一样吃东西？"鱼回答："哦，我看到我的兄弟姐妹吃得越多，它们消失得就越快。"

寓意：从他人的"成功"里学到经验。

Taking It a Step Further——Moral Prompts

* Can you name five successful people who are really happy in life? Do they have good marriages and children?

* Being too successful can cause problems, but what kinds of problems are the most common?

Fable 20　The Farmer and the Oxcart

A farmer was taking his rice to the market. The day was very hot. He started to complain to the cart, "Can't you go faster?"

"Sure, I can," replied the oxcart. "But I can't today because you didn't grease my axles. And you didn't straighten my wheels. And you didn't feed the ox."

"You greedy oxcart! You ALWAYS want something," yelled the farmer. "You must learn to obey, and—." But he couldn't continue, because a wheel fell off and the cart tipped over, trapping him under the cart.

寓言 20　　　农夫和牛车

农民正在把他的大米运往市场。那天很热。他开始向牛车抱怨："你不能走快些吗？"

"当然可以。"牛车回答。"但是我今天做不到，因为你没有给我的车轴上润滑油。也没有矫正车轮的方向。你没有喂牛。"

"你真是个贪婪的牛车！你总是想要些东西，"农夫大叫道。"你必须学会遵守。。。"但是他无法继续，因为一只车轮掉了下来，牛车翻倒了，把他压在了下面。

寓意：如果您关照好自己的东西，那么你的事情也会被关照。

Taking It a Step Further——Moral Prompts

* What kinds of things do you maintain?

* A lot of people do not worry about things until they break. Is this smart?

Fable 21   Good for Nothing

An almost blind old dog sat down one evening. He was tired from chasing bats, rats, and cats all day. And the dog knew that his eyes were a real problem. That day he had run into walls, chairs, and tables many times.

The house cat was sitting out up high on the bookcase. She called out to the dog, "You're finished! Good for nothing now! Soon they will kick you out. Finally, I get JUSTICE for all the years of trouble."

"What are YOU complaining about?" replied the dog. He was angry now. "You became strong, limber, watchful, and clever from me chasing you. Without me as your enemy, YOU would be good for nothing."

Moral: Give credit where it is due: recognize the work of others.

寓言 21　　一无是处

一天晚上，一只几近失明的老狗坐在地上。他整日追逐蝙蝠，老鼠和猫，非常疲倦。狗知道他的眼睛是问题的关键。那天，他无数次撞到了墙壁，椅子和桌子。

家猫高高坐在书架上。她对狗喊道，"你完蛋了！现在你是一无是处！很快他们就会把你赶出去。经历了这些年的麻烦，终于，我会得到公正。"

"你在抱怨什么？"那只狗回答。他生气了。"我追逐你，你变得坚强，善于随机应变，警惕和聪明。没有我作为你的敌人，你将一无所获。"

寓意：信誉要公平分享，认可他人的工作。

Taking It a Step Further——Moral Prompts

* Do you think people give you credit for the work that you do?

*Are older people still valued where you live, as they are so worn out like this dog?

Fable 22   The Wolf and The Sheep

Some sheep were walking with their shepherd in the forest. They walked by a wolf. The wolf knew that there was nothing he could do when the shepherd was there. So he called to one sheep, "Gee, I wish I could change and be like a sheep. I really envy you. You are so peaceful. Do you think you could stop and teach me? I am SO tired of being a big bad wolf."

The sheep laughed back. "You cannot be a sheep, just like day cannot be night. And if we stopped, you would be teaching us a lesson. We know that!"

Moral: Your doubts are always the best guide.

寓言 22　　狼和羊

绵羊和他们的牧羊人在森林里散步。他们经过一头狼。狼知道牧羊人在的时候，他无能为力。

于是他对一只绵羊喊道："天哪，我希望我能变成一只绵羊。我真嫉妒你。你太温和了。你可以停下来教教我吗？我非常讨厌成为一只大恶狼。"

羊笑了起来。　"你不能成为绵羊，就像白天不能是黑夜。如果我们停下来，你会让我们学会一个教训。我们知道！"

寓意：怀疑永远是最好的指南。

Taking It a Step Further——Moral Prompts

*Do you have any doubts about anyone or about some situation in your life?

*Do you listen to advice a lot? If so, whose advice do you value the most?

Volume 3

Fable 1　Dancing Cats

Some stray cats were watching the prince. They saw the prince's pet monkeys. The monkeys danced and entertained the people. The people fed the monkeys and loved them. The cats made a plan. They decided to replace the monkeys.

After the monkeys' first act, the cats tied up the monkeys. Then they threw the monkeys under the stage and put on their costumes. The cats meowed and danced, and the people laughed and howled at them. But the prince hated the cats' dancing and went to look for his monkeys.

Moral: *It is easy to imitate.*

寓言 1　跳舞的猫

几只流浪猫在看着王子。他们看到了王子的宠物猴。猴子们跳舞让人们开心。人们就把猴子喂饱，也非常喜欢他们。这些猫制定了计划，他们决定取代猴子们。

在猴子们表演第一幕结束之后，猫群把猴子们绑了起来，然后扔到舞台下面，并穿上了他们的服装。猫们喵喵叫着跳舞，人们大笑着对他们吼叫。可是王子很讨厌猫们的表演，他去寻找猴子们了。

寓意：模仿很容易。

Taking It a Step Further ——Moral Prompts

* Can you imitate or mimic anyone?

* With food, can you tell the difference between something authentic and
something that has been substituted or faked?

Fable 2   Bird Songs

Have you ever thought, "Why do birds sing?" Well, a long time
ago, a bluebird was scratching for worms. She started quietly singing.
The song was so beautiful that it woke up a crow. The crow thought for
a while. Then he decided that he too could sing just as good as the
bluebird. The crow began to caw—slowly and softly at first—and then
louder and faster. He also sang, "I'm the best singer in the forest!"

An eagle was flying in the sky. She heard the crow singing. She
decided that she too could sing. She began to screech even louder,

crying out about her strength, beauty, and intelligence. This led other birds to sing about their own virtues. Even today, the singing has not ended.

Moral: *Jealousy is a noise that is best ignored.*

寓言 2　鸟的歌声

您是否曾经想过，"鸟儿为什么唱歌？"·很久以前，知更鸟正在抓虫子。她开始轻轻地唱歌。歌声太美了，它吵醒了乌鸦。乌鸦想了一会儿。他觉得自己也可以像知更鸟一样美妙地唱歌。乌鸦开始嘶哑地啼叫，缓慢轻柔，然后声音越来大，越来越快。他歌唱着，"我是森林里最好的歌手！"

一只鹰在天上飞过。她听到了乌鸦在唱歌。她觉得自己也可以唱歌。她开始更大声地尖叫，为她的强大，美丽和智慧叫喊。于是，其他鸟类也开始歌唱自己的优点。直到今天，歌唱也没有结束。

寓意：嫉妒是一种最好被忽视的噪音。

Taking It a Step Further——Moral Prompts

* Are you a jealous person? Why or why not?

* Do you consider your friends jealous people? Have they ever shown any jealousy?

Fable 3　Oysters Anyone?

"What are they? They look and smell disgusting," said the black dog to the white dog.

"They're oysters," the white dog replied. "Men eat them so they must be delicious. But they sometimes don't want them. They don't want these oysters either, I guess. Go on, you should eat them. I'm not hungry now."

The black dog started eating the oysters, and the white dog encouraged him. "If some oysters are OK, more oysters must be delicious," he said. Finally, after he had eaten all the oysters, the black dog slowly crawled away. He was very sick with a stomachache from those really spoiled oysters.

Moral: *Some gifts are better not accepted*

寓言 3　有人吃牡蛎吗？

"这些是什么？他们看起来，闻起来都令人恶心。" 黑狗对白狗说。

"它们是牡蛎，" 白狗回答。 "人们吃它们，所以它们一定很美味。但是有时人们也不想吃他们。我猜他们不想要这些牡蛎。来，你可以吃它们。我现在不饿。"

黑狗于是开始吃牡蛎，白狗在鼓励他说，"你看是不是很美味。要是吃得更多，一定更美味。"最后，在吃完所有的牡蛎之后，黑狗慢慢地爬走了。他病得很厉害，吃了变质的牡蛎，肚子很疼。

寓意：有些礼物最好不要接受。

Taking It a Step Further——Moral Prompts

* What kinds of gifts would you rather not receive?

* Is food a good "gift" for you or would you rather receive some object or product

Fable 4　The Wolf and the Sheep Dog

"Oh, how I would like to join you. I can guard sheep too," pleaded a wolf to a sheep dog.

"Hmmm. I don't know. It's your appearance. Your mouth, eyes, and hair make you look too scary," replied the sheep dog.

The wolf begged the dog to help him to have 'not scary' teeth, eyes, and mouth. So, the dog taught the wolf to smile, not to squint, and to comb his hair properly. When they finished, the sheep dog introduced the wolf to his master. The master screamed and chased the wolf from his home.

Moral: *Changing your appearance doesn't change your character.*

寓言 4 狼和牧羊犬

"哦，我真想加入你们的行列！我也可以保护绵羊。" 狼恳求牧羊犬说。

"嗯。我说不好。你的外表，嘴巴，眼睛，还有头发，让你看起来好吓人。" 牧羊犬回答。

狼恳求牧羊犬帮助他有不吓人的牙齿，眼睛和嘴巴。于是，牧羊犬教狼要微笑，不要斜视，并且正确梳理头发。当他们做完这些，牧羊犬把狼介绍给他的主人。主人尖叫着把狼赶出了家门。

寓意：即使改变外表，也不能改变本质。

Taking It a Step Further——Moral Prompts

* If you could change your appearance, what would you change?

* Are women more worried about their appearance than men? If so, why?

Fable 5 Don't Bet on It

"I heard that we have been sold to a new master," said a donkey to a horse. The horse paused, then slowly replied, "So? Will this new master give us oats to eat, larger stalls, less work, and a better life?"

The donkey disagreed, "I am sure things will get better. I have seen this man, and he is tall, good-looking, young, and rich!" The horse chewed his grain for a while and then said, "So. Just because he has a good life doesn't mean that we will have one."

The donkey disagreed and pointed out other wonderful aspects of their new master, but over the next year, his life and the horse's didn't improve. And this is why donkeys are so unhelpful, stubborn, and slow, even today.

Moral: Your feelings may often end up being wrong.

寓言 5　别指望它

"听说我们已经被卖给了新主人。" 驴对马说。马停下来，缓慢地回答："然后呢？这位新主人能给我们提供燕麦，更大的牲畜棚，让我们少工作，更好地生活吗？"

驴不赞成，"我相信情况会好起来的。我见过这个人，他又高又帅，年轻又有钱！" 马嚼了一会儿谷物，然后说："嗯。他有着美好的生活，并不意味着我们也会拥有。"

驴不同意，并指出了新主人在其他方面的优点。但是在接下来的一年里，他和马的生活并没有得到改善。这也是为什么直到今天，驴依然非常无助，固执，行动缓慢。

寓意：你的直觉经常是错误的。

Taking It a Step Further——Moral Prompts

* Are your feelings a better guide for you in life than your ideas and perceptions?

* Do you consider yourself an "emotional" and "sensitive" person? If not, why? If so, how is this shown?

Fable 6   You All Deserve Better

A group of goats and a group of rams met on the side of a mountain. The goats told the rams about how impressed they were by the rams' strength, hair, horns, tails, and white teeth.

The goats added, "You all deserve better grass and greener pastures. There are better pastures up on the top of the mountain, way over there." The rams agreed that they were great creatures. And only great creatures deserve great places. So, they raced up the mountain, leaving the goats with the only green pastures in the land.

Moral: *There is a purpose behind all flattery.*

寓言 6　你值得拥有更好

一群山羊和一群公羊在山边相遇。山羊告诉公羊，它们对公羊的力量，头发，角，尾巴和洁白的牙齿印象深刻。

山羊补充说："你们都值得拥有更好的牧草和更绿的牧场。在山顶上，有更好的牧场，就在那边。"公羊们一致认为他们是伟大的生物。只有伟大的生物，才值得应有好地方。于是，他们飞速奔向山顶，让山羊们独享那片土地上唯一的绿色牧场。

寓意：所有的奉承背后都有目的。

Taking It a Step Further——Moral Prompts

* Do you ever praise anyone?
* Do you like being praised, and if so for what? Your appearance? Your achievements? How you conduct yourself
 relationships?

Fable 7　The House

Two stray dogs walked into an old, empty house. They began looking at all the objects that lay all over the house. The younger dog was puzzled. He began asking his older friend some questions. The older dog told the younger dog all about clocks, tables, clothes, sofas, curtains, pictures, and cupboards.

The younger dog marveled, "I had no idea about people. Why they were richer than I thought. What great creatures they must be." The older dog replied, "If they are so great, why did they leave this house and go away? And why is it such a mess?"

Moral: *Don't leave behind a mess for others to clean up.*

寓言 7　房子

两只流浪狗走进了一间旧的空房子。他们开始观察整个房屋里的所有物件。年轻的小狗感到困惑。他开始问他的老朋友一些问题。年长的狗告诉小狗有关钟表，桌子，衣服，沙发，窗帘，照片和橱柜的所有信息。

小狗惊叹道："我对人一无所知。为什么他们比我想的要富有。他们真是伟大的生物。"年长的狗回答说："如果他们这么伟大，他们为什么离开这所房子离开呢？为什么这里这么乱呢？"

寓意：不要把混乱的场面留给别人收拾。

Taking It a Step Further——Moral Prompts

* Do you clean up after yourself or do your parents do this for you?

* Are women cleaner than men, in general? If so, why?

Fable 8　Learning About Golf

A group of animals were resting deep in the forest. "Man is doing it again," said the stork. "The crows told me something. He's now hitting small, white eggs up in the air and chasing after them."

"SEE! SEE! I told you that man is crazy!" shouted the blue jay. "Imagine hitting someone's eggs."

"I heard that man is using long metal clubs to hit the eggs," said the duck. "Well, he is NOT getting near my eggs."

"Maybe man is simply hitting the eggs over to a place where he can eat them better," said the snake. The discussion continued. Soon the animals were so afraid that none of them ever laid another egg.

Moral: *Fear of hardship is often worse than hardship itself.*

寓言 8　学习打高尔夫

一群动物在森林深处休息。"人类又来了。"鹳说："乌鸦告诉我，人类把空中的白色小鸡蛋打碎，然后追赶它们。"

"看！看！我告诉过你人类疯了！"蓝鸦叫着。"想想他们会打碎别人的蛋。"

"我听说人类用长的金属棒去打碎蛋，"鸭子说："还好，他们没有靠近我的蛋。"

"也许人类只是把蛋打到一个地方，他们可以安心食用。"蛇说。

讨论在继续。很快，动物们太害怕了，于是他们都不下蛋了。

寓意：面对困难的恐惧往往比困难本身更难以克服。

Taking It a Step Further——Moral Prompts

* Do you ever worry about any kind of future "hardship"? If so, what do you worry about the most?

* What kind of past events have been the hardest on you? What have you learned from them?

Fable 9 The Contest

Some hornets, wasps, flies, bees, and mosquitoes came together. They were arguing about which one caused man the most problems. All of the insects felt that they were the worst pest. So, they decided on a contest. They would all pester one family for one day. However, the winner was soon decided.

The family's flowers distracted the bees. The family's food distracted the flies. And the hornets and wasps were more interested in making their homes in the man's chimney. Only the mosquitoes pestered the family all day long.

Moral: *Determination, not strength, often makes the difference.*

寓言 9 竞赛

马蜂，黄蜂，苍蝇，蜜蜂和蚊子聚在一起。他们在争论到底是誰给人类造成了最大问题。所有的昆虫都觉得自己是最可恶的害虫。因此，他们决定进行一场竞赛。他们会分别纠缠一家人一整天。但是，获胜者很快就确定了。

那一家的花分散了蜜蜂的注意力。食物又吸引了苍蝇。马蜂和黄蜂更有兴趣在烟囱里安家。一整天只有蚊子不停地骚扰一家人。

寓意：决心而不是能力起关键作用。

* What are you really determined about, that is what are the most important goals for you?

* Who is the most determined person in your family? Why?

Fable 10   We Changed Our Minds

A long time ago, Mother Nature felt sorry for the frogs and the moles because they were weakest of all animals. She said to them, "You can change one thing about yourselves."

The frogs said, "We frogs want a normal tongue so we can talk the cranes out of eating us." The moles, in turn, said, "We moles wish for bigger eyes, so we can see the danger in front of us." After one month, the frogs and moles appeared before Mother Nature again.

This time they begged her to change them back to the way they were before. "Please, please change us back," they said. "We changed our minds." The frogs had learned that speech was useless because the cranes didn't want to listen. The moles realized that seeing dangerous animals only made them more nervous.

Moral: *What is most truly valuable is often not appreciated.*

寓言 10　我们改变了主意

很久以前，大自然母亲一直为青蛙和鼹鼠感到遗憾，因为它们是所有动物中最弱小的。她对他们说："你们可以改变自己的一个特征。"

青蛙们说："我们青蛙想要普通的舌头，这样我们就可以劝说仙鹤不要吃我们了。"

轮到鼹鼠了。他们说，"我们鼹鼠希望有更大的眼睛，这样我们就可以看到前方的危险。"

一个月后，青蛙和鼹鼠再次出现在大自然母亲面前。

这次，他们恳求她，把他们改回从前的样子。"恳求您了，请把我们变回去吧。"他们说，"我们改变了主意。"青蛙们明白了会说话是没有用的，因为仙鹤们根本不想听。鼹鼠们意识到，看到危险的动物在眼前只会令它们更加紧张。

寓意：真正有价值的东西经常不被欣赏。

Taking It a Step Further ——Moral Prompts

* What do you appreciate the most about your life and your own possessions? Why?

* What is the most valuable object that you own?

Fable 11   The Plotters

Several young rabbits, rats, foxes, snakes, pigs, and birds came together. They were plotting how to overthrow the lion, the King of the Jungle. They all felt he was a cruel tyrant. There were so many plans. So, they called on the tortoise to decide which plan was best. The tortoise was the oldest and wisest creature among them.

The animals told the tortoise about their 'new and fail-proof' plans based on nighttime raids, rabbit decoys, and foxes disguise. Then the tortoise motioned for the discussion to end.

He said, "You all had better just go home. I've heard ALL of these ideas before. In fact, I hear them every ten years or so! AND every single time, the lion is never overthrown, and the plotters are all eaten."

Moral: *It's hard to have new ideas.*

寓言 11   阴谋家

几只小兔子，老鼠，狐狸，蛇，猪和鸟聚集在一起。他们正在密谋如何打倒丛林之王狮子。他们都觉得他是一个暴君。计划太多了。所以，他们让乌龟来决定哪个计划最好。乌龟是所有动物里，年龄最大，最聪明的生物。

动物们向乌龟讲述了他们根据夜间突袭制定的"万无一失新计划"，兔子做诱饵，狐狸去伪装。接着乌龟让他们中止了讨论。

他说："你们最好还是回家吧。我以前也听说过所有这些想法。实际上，每隔十年左右，我就会听到一次！而且每一次，狮子不会被推翻，但是阴谋者们却都被吃掉了。"

寓意：想要有新的想法，很不容易。

Taking It a Step Further——Moral Prompts

* What have been some new ideas that you have had lately?

* Do people appreciate your "new ideas"?

Fable 12   The Collection

An old mole walked by a dump and to his surprise, saw a pile of glass bottles, cups, balls, and beads. The glass sparkled and shined in the sunlight. The mole could even see his own face in the glass. And when he touched the glass, the mole found it as smooth as water.

The mole decided that he just had to take these objects of beauty to his burrow. One by one, he dragged or carried each one to his home. At the entrance of his tunnel under a large tree, he pushed each item down into his burrow. He was sure that they would light up his dark life.

He muttered to himself, "Ahhh....with these beautiful things, I am the richest mole in the world. I will be the ENVY of the forest." However, when he finished and entered his burrow, he found many of the glass pieces were broken, and the others were dark and dull.

Moral: *Selfishness will take the shine off of any collection.*

寓言 12　收藏品

老鼹鼠从垃圾旁走过，他惊奇地发现一堆玻璃瓶，杯子，球和珠子。玻璃在阳光下闪闪发光。鼹鼠甚至在玻璃中看到了自己的脸。当他触摸玻璃时，鼹鼠感到它像水一样光滑。

鼹鼠决定把这些美丽的物件带回他的洞穴中。他一个接一个地拖着，抬着回到了家。在一棵大树下的隧道入口处，他把这些物件都推入了洞穴。他确信这些东西会照亮他的黑暗生活。

他自言自语道："啊…有了这些美丽的东西，我就是世界上最富有的鼹鼠。我将被整个森林嫉妒。"可是，当他进入洞穴，发现很多玻璃都被打碎了，剩下的一些则变得暗淡无光。

寓意：自私会让任何收藏品失去光泽。

Taking It a Step Further——Moral Prompts

* What kind of objects attract your own attention?

* Are there any possessions that you own that you would have a hard time sharing?

Fable 13   A Pig's Life

A parrot saw a pig wallowing in a pit. The parrot began to lecture the pig about the virtues of work. "You are wasting your time," said the parrot. "You had better get out and work. If you don't work, you will never have any self-respect." At first, the pig didn't listen to the parrot. But he finally agreed and began to inquire about vocations. He read the job advertisements posted by a farmer.

1. Truffle Finder. Must be able to smell and locate easily these valuable and rare mushrooms. The pig thought, "No, I would be wasting my energy. Truffles are too rare. There just aren't enough truffles to earn a REAL living."

2. Breeder. Must be fertile, energetic, and good looking. Again, the pig thought, "Looks like a dead-end job to me. I would be wasting my time."

3. Pig Racer. Applicants must be able to run in circles and consistently win. Experience required.

The pig sighed, "Hmmm....no, no, this won't do either. I would be wasting my talents. I wouldn't be appreciated." In the end, the pig didn't choose a job and stayed wallowing in the pit.

Moral: *The lazy have the most excuses.*

寓言 13　猪的一生

鹦鹉看到猪在坑里打滚。鹦鹉开始向猪讲述有关工作的美德。"你在浪费时间。"鹦鹉说，"你最好出去工作。如果你不工作，你将永远不会有自尊心。"一开始，猪没有听鹦鹉在说什么。但是最终他同意鹦鹉的建议，并且开始询问职业的事情。他读到了农民张贴的招工广告。

1.　　松露搜寻员。要求必须嗅觉灵敏，并轻松找到这些稀有的蘑菇。猪在想："不，这样我会浪费我的精力。松露太少有了。找松露不能让我足以谋生。"

2. 繁殖人员。要求繁殖能力强，精力充沛，长相好看。猪又在想："对我来说，像是一个没有前途的工作。简直是浪费我的时间。"

3.猪竞技选手。申请人必须能够绕圈奔跑并且持续获胜。要求有竞技经验。猪叹了口气："嗯。。。不，不，这也不行。这会浪费我的才华。没有人会赞赏我。"

最后，猪没有选择任何工作，继续呆在坑里打滚。

寓意：懒惰的人最有理由。

Taking It a Step Further——Moral Prompts

* Do you know of any lazy people that always have excuses for not doing something or achieving their goals?

* What is the best way of dealing with lazy people?

Fable 14 Charms for Sale

A peddler was selling "lucky" things. He had glass balls, rabbits' feet, medals, and wands. When no one bought anything, he cried out, "Discount" and "Sale." He wanted to attract customers. He also told passers-by, "These items have given much luck, love, and adventure to their previous owners. The girl who owned this rabbit's foot became a famous violin player. The owner of this medal traveled all over the world!"

A boy asked, "Why are you selling them if they are so powerful? Why don't you keep them?" The peddler replied, "Child, I need MONEY, not luck, adventure, or love."

Moral: *Necessity overpowers all superstition.*

寓言 14　贩卖吉祥

小商贩在叫卖能带来好运气的吉祥物，有玻璃球，兔子的脚，奖牌和魔杖。看到没有人买任何东西，他开始叫喊："折扣出售。"他想吸引顾客。他还对路过的人说："这些物品给以前的主人带来了很多好运气，爱和冒险的经历。拥有这只兔子脚的女孩成为了著名的小提琴演奏家。这块勋章的拥有者曾经环游了世界！"

一个男孩问："既然它们这么厉害，你为什么要卖掉它们？你为什么不自己保留？"小商贩回答说："孩子，我需要钱，而不是运气，爱或是冒险的经历。"

寓意：必要性比任何迷信令人折服。

Taking It a Step Further——Moral Prompts

* What do you need in life? Love? Money? Adventure? Luck?

* Do you believe in any lucky "amulets" or objects?

* Do you avoid any and all superstitious beliefs?

Fable 15　Easy Way or Hard Way

A pigeon was slowly building her nest, stick by stick. A crow flew by. "Oh, you are doing that the hard way," the crow said. "Sticks are too small. You should use twigs. Here, I will show you."

The crow then snapped off a huge twig from a nearby branch. He rammed the twig into the pigeon's nest, almost destroying it. So the pigeon started trying to use twigs to build her nest.

As she struggled to break and carry off more twigs, an eagle landed. "You're doing that the hard way," advised the eagle. "Grass is much better for building nests. It's much easier."

The pigeon then learned from a crane that using flowers was even easier. Later a vulture advised that using bones made things much stronger and was far easier.

At the end of the day, the pigeon realized that twigs were too hard to carry, grass rotted, flowers faded, and bones stunk. It was better to just use sticks to build her nest. She decided to do what she had been doing all along.

Moral: *Finding the easiest way is the hard way.*

寓言 15　容易还是难

鸽子在用一根根的木棍，慢慢地筑巢。一只乌鸦飞过。"哦，你的方法太慢了。"乌鸦说，"木棍太小了。你应该用树枝。来，我告诉你怎么办。"

然后，乌鸦从附近的树上衔来一个大树枝。他把树枝强行塞进了鸽子窝，差点儿把它折断。于是，鸽子开始尝试用树枝筑巢。

当她努力折断树枝，并把他们叼过去的时候，老鹰出现了。"你的方法太慢了。"老鹰建议说，"用草来筑巢会更好。这要容易得多。"

　　接着，鸽子又从仙鹤那儿得知，用鲜花筑巢会更省力。后来，秃鹰又建议可以用骨头来筑巢，这样更坚固，也更容易。

　　最终，鸽子意识到树枝难以携带，草容易腐烂，鲜花会枯萎，骨头发臭令人作呕。用木棍筑巢是最好的办法。她决定用一直以来自己使用的方法筑巢。

寓意：寻找最容易的办法，其实是最难的。

Taking It a Step Further——Moral Prompts

* What do you need in life? Love? Money? Adventure? Luck?
* Do you believe in any lucky "amulets" or objects?

Fable 16 The Olive Tree and the Fig Tree

An olive tree and a fig tree were growing very close together. They began to fight about their own share of sunlight, space, and water. One day their argument got so bad that each tried to hurt the other.

The fig tree splattered rotten figs on the bark of the olive tree so that birds would peck at it. In response, the olive tree began to block off the rainwater.

In turn, the fig tree stretched its branches so that the olive tree got no sunlight at all. Later that year, a man walked by, and he barely noticed the two dwarfed, bent, and ugly trees. He didn't even know what they were.

Moral: *Revenge gets you nowhere.*

寓言 16　橄榄树和无花果树

橄榄树和无花果树紧靠着生长在一起。他们开始为拥有更多的阳光，空间和水而争斗。有一天，他们的争吵特别剧烈，以至于都试图伤害对方。

无花果树把腐烂的无花果甩到橄榄树的树皮上，于是很多鸟飞来啄食。作为回应，橄榄树开始阻挡雨水。

随后，无花果树伸展了枝叶，橄榄树就完全得不到阳光。那一年晚些时候，一个男人走了过来。他几乎没有注意到这两棵矮小，弯曲和丑陋的树。他甚至不知道它们是什么。

寓意：报复毫无意义。

Taking It a Step Further——Moral Prompts
* Do you ever "win" at arguments with your friends or family?
* Why do you think people argue so much in life instead of "talking things out" with each other?

Fable 17　Trampoline Time

"My web is like a trampoline. It's here for you all! Please, please, come and bounce around on it," said a spider to a group of ladybugs.

"But, we may fall off of it," said one.

"It's too dangerous," added another.

The spider laughed, "No, that won't be a problem, I assure you. Please come." But the ladybugs then expressed other worries about the web.

"The strings are too thin," said one ladybug.

"They're not good quality," said another.

"And they're too old," added a third.

"They're not clean, either," complained another.

"And they won't last long," added yet another.

"And they really aren't very strong," said one more.

"And…"

"Enough!" yelled the spider. He became impatient and crawled away. He said angrily to himself, "Without a doubt such JOYLESS and worried bugs would never be tasty."

Moral: *Caution can save you from many problems.*

寓言 17　蹦床时间

"我的网就像蹦床。它就在这儿！为你们所有人！来吧，来吧，让我们一起跳起来。"蜘蛛对一群瓢虫说。

"但是，我们会从上面掉下去。"一只瓢虫说。

"这太危险了。"另一只补充道。

蜘蛛笑着说："不，那根本不是问题，我敢保证。过来吧。"可是瓢虫们对蜘蛛网还是又很多担心。

"网线太细了。"一只瓢虫说。

"它们的质量不太好。"另一只说。

"而且它们太旧了。"第三只补充到。

"它们也不干净。"还有一只抱怨说。

"它们用不了多久就会坏。"又一只接着说。

"他们太不结实了。"还有一只说。

"嗯…"

"够了！"蜘蛛大喊。他不耐烦地爬走了。他生气地对自己说："毫无疑问，这些不欢乐，忧虑重重的虫子们一定不好吃。"

寓意：小心谨慎会让你远离麻烦。

Taking It a Step Further——Moral Prompts

* Do you know of any complainers in your own life? What do they complain about?

* When someone complains to you about something you have done, how do you feel?

Fable 18 Presents

A fox sent a present of some tasty frogs and mice to a crane. The crane expressed his hearty thanks. So, the fox sent more presents of fish, crickets, and snails to the crane.

One cold, snowy day, the fox came to visit the crane. "You know, I'm kind of hungry," the fox said. "It's been hard for the past few days, and I haven't caught anything. Do you have any food for me? Roast squirrel would be fine."

The crane replied, "Oh, fox, I have no such food."

"Perhaps a baked rabbit or two?" inquired the fox.

"No, we, cranes do not dine on rabbits," answered the crane.

"Ah, what a shame," replied the fox, smiling. "But as you are now fat from my many presents, I guess I have to dine on you."

Moral: *The gifts from those of evil repute are not free.*

寓言18 礼物

狐狸把几只美味的青蛙和老鼠当作礼物送给了仙鹤。仙鹤对此表达了由衷的感谢。于是，狐狸又送给仙鹤更多的鱼，蟋蟀和蜗牛。

一天，天很冷，还在下着雪。狐狸去拜访仙鹤。狐狸说："你知道，我有点饿。过去这几天很艰难，我什么都没有捕捉到。你有食物分给我吗？有烤松鼠就太好了。"

仙鹤回答说："哦，狐狸先生，我没有这样的食物。"

"有一两只兔子也可以啊。"狐狸又说。

仙鹤回答："不，我们仙鹤不吃兔子。"

"啊，那可惜了。"狐狸微笑着回答说。"但是你吃了我的很多礼物，现在足够胖了，我想我只能吃掉你了。"

寓意：名声不好的人从来都不会送免费的礼物。

Taking It a Step Further——Moral Prompts

* Do you know of any complainers in your own life? What do they complain about?

* When someone complains to you about something you have done, how do you feel?

Fable 19   Let's Go —

Two cockroaches were lying in wait to raid the kitchen table. The younger and more enthusiastic roach kept urging his older brother to move. "Come on. Let's go! We're wasting time. It's safe! What are you worried about?"

The older cockroach was overwhelmed by such enthusiasm, and finally agreed. As the two raced to the food, a woman stepped out of the shadows and squashed them.

Moral: *Enthusiasm alone will take you nowhere.*

寓言 19   我们走吧！

两只蟑螂躺在地上等待突袭厨房的餐桌。年轻小一些，更有热情的蟑螂不断敦促他的哥哥快点走。"来呀！我们走吧！我们在浪费时间。现在很安全！你担心什么？"

年长的蟑螂被弟弟的热情征服，最终同意了。当两只蟑螂奔向食物的时侯，一个女人从阴影里走出，并将他们压扁。

寓意：只有热情是不会成功的。

Taking It a Step Further——Moral Prompts

* Do you think that the more enthusiastic you are about something, the less careful you become?

* Do you really think through all of your plans? Do you find it difficult to foresee possible problems and issues?

Fable 20   Birds of a Feather

As a crow was walking to a lake, he passed by various birds. All the birds insulted the crow.

"Look at that nasty creature," said a crane.

"Garbage-eater," yelled out a swan.

"Low-life parasite," added a bluebird.

"Bad DNA there," cautioned a finch to his children. An eagle overheard the remarks. She later flew down to check up on the crow. She found the crow happy, and completely unperturbed.

"Why aren't you bothered by those insults?" the eagle asked.

"Well, I can't change the other birds, but I can change how I feel. And I want to feel GOOD! So, it's easier to just forgive and forget."

Moral: *Insults are best ignored.*

寓言 20　一丘之貉

一只乌鸦走向湖边。各种鸟类从他身边经过，所有的鸟都侮辱他。

"看看那个令人讨厌的家伙。" 仙鹤说。

"他只配吃垃圾。" 天鹅大喊到。

"下流的寄生虫"。蓝鸟补充说。

"那儿有个恶劣的人。" 朱雀警告他的孩子们。

老鹰听到了这些话。于是她飞下来查看乌鸦。她发现乌鸦非常愉快，并没有受到打扰。

"你为什么没有被那些侮辱所困扰？"老鹰问。

"嗯，我改变不了别的鸟，但是我可以改变自己的感觉。我想让自己开心！所以，原谅和忘记就变得很容易。"

寓意：被侮辱时，最好不去理会。

Taking It a Step Further ——Moral Prompts

* Have you ever been insulted in your life? Was it easy for you to ignore such insults?

* Do you know of any bullies? How did you react to them?

Fable 21   The Robbers

Two robbers came across a camp of merchants. The merchants were all asleep, exhausted from their journey. Four mules were tied up to a tree. Two of the mules had very heavy bags. The robbers quickly decided that these mules carried jewels, gold, and money. So, they untied the two mules and silently left with them.

The robbers, however, found that their escape was slow. The mules were tired and slow. Eventually, the robbers untied the bags and took them off the mules. They left the mules and carried the bags themselves for a few hours. Exhausted, they found a cave. They eagerly opened the bags, only to find nails, nuts, and bolts.

Moral: *Being too greedy can bring you disappointment.*

寓言 21　强盗

两个强盗来到了一群商人聚集的营地。商人们精疲力尽，全都睡着了。四只骡子被栓在了一棵树上。两只骡子驮着很重的袋子。强盗们很快判断出这些骡子在驮着珠宝，黄金和钱。因此，他们牵着把两只骡子，悄悄地离开了。

但是，强盗们发现他们逃跑的速度太慢。骡子们太累了，跑不快。最后，强盗们把袋子从骡子身上取下，自己背着。他们甩开了骡子，背了几个小时，精疲力竭的时候，发现了一个山洞。当他们热切地打开袋子时，只看到了里面的钉子，螺母和螺栓。

寓意：过于贪婪的人容易失望。

Taking It a Step Further——Moral Prompts

* Do you know of anyone that is greedy?

* Do you think that owning a lot of things makes you happy in the end?

Fable 22 The Egret and the Elephant

In Africa, an egret was enjoying feeding in a marsh when an elephant came up and started splashing around, drinking and bathing in the water. It wasn't long after that several other elephants joined him, causing a ruckus.

The egret chirped at the elephants, "EXCUSE ME, but I am afraid this marsh belongs to ME. You all just can't come in here dirtying up the water and disturbing everything and scaring away the fish here. HOW am I to EAT with all of this noise?"

To the egret's great surprise, the elephants completely ignored the egret and continued to bath and splash water on each other, causing even more noise.

The egret was incensed. "HELLO! ANYONE HOME? AS I SAID BEFORE, this marsh is MINE! Now leave."

The bull elephant then raised its trunk and said, "We heard you the first time. And we think you are all wet." And then the elephant blew a torrent of water on the egret causing it to fly away.

Moral: *Few have the time or energy to listen to selfishness.*

寓言 22　白鹭和大象

在非洲，当白鹭正享受着在沼泽中觅食，一头大象飞奔而来。水四处飞溅，大象又是喝水，又是沐浴。很快，又有几只大象加入到他的行列，引起一阵骚动。

白鹭对着大象唧唧叫着，"对不起，可是这片沼泽属于我。你们不能跑到这里，弄脏了水，吓跑了鱼，打扰周围的人。这么嘈杂，我该如何吃东西？"

令白鹭大吃一惊的是这些大象对白鹭完全置之不理。他们继续洗澡，把水溅到彼此的身上，制造了更大的噪音。

白鹭被激怒了。"喂！有人听到了吗？我说过，这个沼泽是我的！现在马上离开！"

公象扬抬了他的长鼻子，说："我们第一次就听到你说了。我们觉得你身上一定湿透了。"然后，大象鼻子喷出了一股洪流，白鹭不得不飞走了。

Taking It a Step Further ——Moral Prompts

* Do you know of any really selfish people? Why do you think that they became this way?

* How do you deal with selfish people?

Volume 4

Fable 1   A Cat's Dinner

A small cat saw a crow. It decided that the crow would make a nice meal and caught it. The crow begged for mercy. "Please, please, Mr. Cat. I have a family and a job. I'm an important member in my community."

But the cat didn't listen. After its meal, the cat wandered into a clearing for a nap. While it slept, a large vulture landed. Thinking the cat was dead, the vulture pounced on it.

The cat begged for mercy, talking about its family, job, and community service. But the vulture interrupted, "Well I hope all of that makes you tastier."

Moral: *Don't expect kindness unless you can give it.*

寓言 1　猫的晚餐

一只小猫看见了一只乌鸦。它决定把乌鸦做成一顿美餐，于是抓住了乌鸦。乌鸦求饶说，"求求您了，猫先生。我有家庭和工作。我是我们社区中的重要成员。"

但是猫没有听。吃完饭后，它漫步到一个林间的空地小憩。猫打盹的时候，飞来一只秃鹫。秃鹫觉得猫已经死了，就突然猛向它。

猫恳求怜悯，谈论起它的家庭，工作和社区服务。但是秃鹫打断它说，"我希望所有这些都会让你更美味。"

寓意：除非你能给予别人同样的善良，否则不要期待。

Taking It a Step Further ——Moral Prompts

* Have you ever been really angry at someone? What happened?

* Can you still be kind to someone who has treated you badly?

Fable 2　How About a Ride?

A poor traveler, who was tired, saw a beautiful black stallion. The traveler asked the stallion if he could ride it to the next town. But the stallion kicked up its heels and said, "Only a man with good training can ride me. And that man will need to bring me a few treats. I want some carrots, oats, and apples. And the man must have the best equipment for me, too."

The traveler didn't have any training. And he didn't have any treats or equipment, either. So, he continued on until he saw a donkey. Again, he begged for a ride.

"Oh donkey, I don't have any treats, training, and equipment, but could you take me to the next town?" asked the traveler.

"Sure, no problem," replied the donkey. And the donkey carried the traveler to the next town.

Moral: *The lowest are often more generous than the high and mighty.*

寓言 2　驮我一程，好吗？

一个可怜的旅行者，在疲惫不堪的时候，看到了一匹漂亮的黑色牡马。旅行者问牡马是否可以驮他到下一个城镇。但是牡马踢了一下它的后蹄，说："只有受过良好训练的人才能骑我。那个人还需要带给我一些好吃的东西。我想要一些胡萝卜，燕麦和苹果。而且他还必须为我提供最好的装备。"旅行者没有接受过任何训练，而且他也没有任何可以款待牡马的食物和装备。于是，他继续前行，直到他看到了一头驴。他再一次恳求驴可以驮他。

"亲爱的驴子，我没有可以款待你的食物，没有经过训练，也没有马匹装备。但是您能带我去下一个城镇吗？"旅行者问。

"当然可以，没问题。"驴子回答。接着，驴子把旅行者驮到了下一个城镇。

寓意：地位低的人往往比地位高，有能力的人慷慨。

Taking It a Step Further ——Moral Prompts

* Do you feel that people who are richer are less kind?

* Has someone who is poorer than you be nicer to you than other people?

Fable 3 The Deer and the Fawn

A young fawn looked deep into her mother's eyes and said, "I finally understand why those dogs and hunters want you so much. Your eyes are like precious gems. Your lips are sweet. And your fur, warmth, and love are priceless. They want you because of your beauty, don't they, mother?"

The deer replied, "I don't think those hunters appreciate my better qualities, my daughter."

"Perhaps," replied the fawn, "they want you because of your strength and speed. You are so fast."

"No, my daughter, I don't think the hunters think about my strength and speed."

The fawn persisted. "It must be because of your gentle nature, and the peace you give to others." The deer chewed some grass and thought for a while. Then she said, "Yes, my daughter, that's right. It seems that my peaceful and gentle nature really bothers them when I eat their crops and tear down their fences."

Moral: *Actions will—in the end—always show who is really good.*

寓言 3　母鹿和小鹿

一只小鹿深深地凝望着母亲的眼睛，说道："我终于明白了为什么那些狗和猎人那么想得到您。您的眼睛像珍贵的宝石。您的嘴唇看起来非常甜美。而您的皮毛，温暖的气质，还有爱是无价的。他们想得到您，是因为您的美丽，对吧，妈妈？"

母鹿回答说："我不认为那些猎人欣赏我出众的气质，我的女儿。"

小鹿答道："也许，因为他们想得到您，是因为您的强壮和奔跑的速度。您跑得太快了。"

"不，我的女儿，我不认为猎人们在意我的强壮和奔跑的速度。"

小鹿坚持说："那一定是因为您的温柔天性，以及给予他人的平和。"

母鹿嚼了些草，想了一会儿，然后说："是的，我的女儿，是这样。看样子，当我吃掉农作物，踢毁栅栏时，我的温柔和平和确实令他们困扰。"

寓意：行动会最终证明，什么才是真正地好。

Taking It a Step Further ——Moral Prompts

* Have you met people who say that they are "good" people but have shown in their behavior that they are not?

* How do you know if someone is really good?

Fable 4   The Two Rivers and the Sea

Two rivers joined together and ran into the sea. They soon realized that their water was not tasty and drinkable anymore. They complained to the sea, "When we were rivers, we kept ourselves clean. If you kept yourself clean, this wouldn't have happened."

The sea's pride was hurt. It replied, "I've given up being clean. It's vain and stupid. I'm all about depth and size. And you both are here to increase them. In short, you are both here for me. I am obviously all that matters in this world."

Moral: *Those who are big often do not understand and appreciate the small.*

寓言 4　两条河和大海

两条河流汇合在一起，流入大海。然后，他们很快就意识到他们的水不再美味，不能再被饮用了。他们向大海抱怨说："当我们是河流时，我们保持自己的清洁。如果你也能保持清洁，就不会有这样的事情发生。"

大海的自尊心受到了伤害。它回答说："我已经放弃了保持清洁。那是徒劳和愚蠢的。我只关心深度和规模。你们加入我，就是为了提升这两个指标。简单地说，你们在这儿，是为了成全我。很显然，我才是这个世界上最重要的。"

寓意：有权势的人通常不理解，不欣赏卑微的人。

Taking It a Step Further ——Moral Prompts

* Do some adults not appreciate you?

* Do you think that rich or famous people know what it is like for the "common people"?

Fable 5 The Boy and the Knife

A boy was cutting some cheese when the knife he was holding slipped and cut his hand. He ran to his mother, crying.

His mother looked at his hand and laughed. "My son," she said, "a knife is like a person. It can be sharp and hurt you unless you know how to hold it right. Next time, grasp it firmly, with some conviction. Know what you are going to do with it, and then be careful. If you do this, all will be well, and you and the knife will get along just fine."

Moral: *Conviction and confidence will help you to avoid any cuts and bruises that life may toss in your direction.*

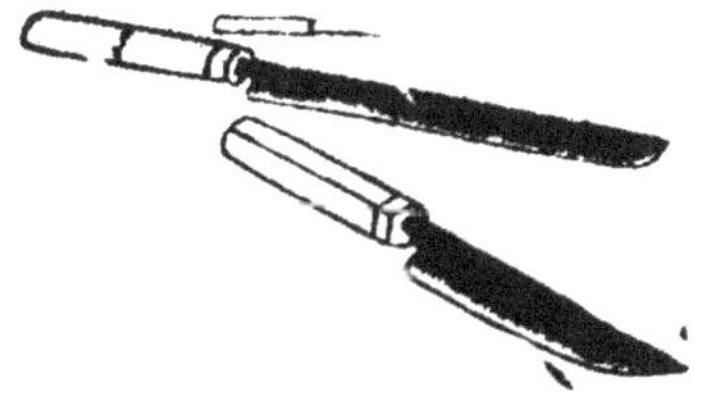

寓言5　男孩和刀

小男孩正握着刀切奶酪，可是手滑，切到了自己的手。他哭着跑向妈妈。

妈妈看着他的手，笑了。她说："我的儿子，刀就像一个人。除非您知道如何正确握住它，否则它很锋利，可能伤害到你。下次，紧紧抓住，坚定地去切。要知道你用它来干什么，然后要小心操作。如果这样做的话，不会有问题，你也会和刀愉快相处。"

寓意：坚定和信心会帮助你躲避生活甩给你的任何创伤。

Taking It a Step Further ——Moral Prompts

* Do you have enough confidence? What are you the most unsure about? Is it math? Physical activities?

* What is the best way to gain confidence?

Fable 6　The Hunter and the Fisherman

A hunter met a fisherman in the forest. The fisherman was bringing home a basket filled with fish. The hunter was bringing home some ducks. They started talking and decided that it would be good to make a trade. Each could enjoy some other type of meat.

"I'll give you one fish for one duck," suggested the fisherman.

"What?" replied the hunter. "It's easy to catch a fish. I had to work hard to get just one duck. For one duck, I need three fish."

"Three fish? That's unbelievable. It took me an hour to get just one fish. These rivers are all fished out. It's hard to get a good-sized fish now." The two continued arguing but were never able to make a trade.

Moral: *Your own labor is rarely appreciated by others.*

寓言 6 猎人和渔夫

一位猎人在森林里遇见了一位渔夫。渔夫正在把装满鱼的篮子带回家。猎人在把一些鸭子带回家。他们开始交谈，并决定进行一项交易。这样两个人都可以享用到其他种类的肉。

"我给你一条鱼换一只鸭子。" 渔夫提议说。

"什么？" 猎人回答。"钓鱼很容易。抓到一只鸭子却很费劲。我需要三条鱼换一只鸭子。"

"三条鱼？真是难以置信。我花了一个小时才钓到一条鱼。这些河都被捞空了。现在很难钓到大鱼了。" 两人继续争论，可是从没有能够进行一笔交易。

寓意：你的努力很少会得到别人的认可。

Taking It a Step Further ——Moral Prompts

* Do some adults not appreciate you?

* Do you think that rich or famous people know what it is like for the "common people"?

Fable 7 The Old Lion

An old, crippled lion lay down in the bush. A buffalo saw the lion. She remembered when the lion attacked her children. She ran and gave the lion a good stomping.

Then a boar rushed up to get revenge for a long-ago injury. An antelope then came up and pierced the lion for chasing her herd.

A man saw all the other animals succeed in their attempts to hurt the lion. He decided to join in, and as he rushed up to the lion, it turned and roared. The man turned and quickly ran away along with the other animals.

Moral: *Success in a few cases doesn't mean success in all cases.*

寓言 7　老狮子

　　一只瘸腿的老狮子躺倒在灌木丛里。一头水牛看见了狮子。她还记得狮子袭击她的孩子们的情景。她跑过去，重重地踩在狮子身上。

　　接着，一头公猪也冲上去，为自己很长时间以前的受伤报仇。然后一只羚羊跑过来，用羊角刺穿了狮子，因为它曾经追赶羊群。

　　有一个人看到所有动物都成功地伤害了狮子。他决定加入其中。当他冲向狮子的时候，狮子转过身并咆哮起来。这个人迅速转身，和其他动物一起逃跑了。

寓意：一些成功的案例并不意味着永远如此。

Taking It a Step Further ——Moral Prompts

* What subjects are you the most successful in? Did you ever get frustrated by any particular class or teacher?

* Do you think as you get older, that you will find it easier to succeed or do you think the competition will just make things more difficult for you?

Fable 8   The Hunter and the Lion

Two hunters were following the tracks of a lion. One hunter was skilled and one was young and just learning how to hunt. The skilled hunter told his friend to follow the lion's tracks while he went out to scout around.

The skilled hunter went up to the top of the mountain. He found no lions or any animals. So he returned to his companion. The young hunter was sitting down. "Why are you sitting here?" exclaimed his friend. "I told you to follow those tracks and find that lion."

"Well, I did. I did what you told me. But the tracks stopped right here at this tree. I didn't know what to do next, so I sat right down here." The skilled hunter froze. He slowly looked up to see the lion snarling down at him.

Moral: The hunter can easily become the hunted.

寓言 8   猎人和狮子

两名猎人正在追踪一头狮子。其中一位猎人技艺娴熟，另一位比较年轻，正在学习如何狩猎。技艺熟练的猎人告诉他的朋友，当他出去四下侦察的时候，要跟随狮子的足迹，技艺熟练的猎人登上了山顶。他没有发现狮子或是任何动物。于是他回去找到了同伴。年轻的猎人正坐在地上。"你为什么坐在这里？" 他的朋友大声问。"我告诉过你，要沿着那些足迹，去寻找狮子。"

"嗯，我找了。我照你说的做了，但是狮子的足迹就在这棵树下，没有了。我不知道下一步该怎么做，所以我就坐在这儿。" 技艺熟练的猎人身体僵硬。他慢慢抬起头，看到了狮子正在向他咆哮。

寓意：猎人很容易成为猎物。

Taking It a Step Further ——Moral Prompts

* What kind of situations have you seen in which someone who was   in charge suddenly lost power?

* Do powerful people seem too arrogant to you sometimes?

Fable 9   The Swollen Husband

A husband and wife decided to stop at a hamburger restaurant. The wife looked at her husband's big stomach. She told him, "I will get a double cheeseburger for myself. And I'll get fries, a salad, a shake, and a dessert. You will just get water." The husband howled in protest, but his wife held up his hand.

"Until you lose those hamburgers from last week, last month, and last year, you won't get any more."

Moral: *Those who have too much often still want more.*

寓言 9　身材臃肿的丈夫

夫妻俩决定在一家汉堡餐厅用餐。妻子看着丈夫的大肚子，告诉他说："我会为自己买一个双层芝士汉堡。然后我会吃炸薯条，沙拉，奶昔和甜点。你就喝点水吧。" 丈夫大声抗议，但妻子举起手，捂住了他的嘴。

"直到你减掉上周，上个月和去年你吃过的那些汉堡。反正你不能再吃了。"

寓意：已经得到太多的人，还是想要更多。

（贪婪的人永无止境。）

Taking It a Step Further ——Moral Prompts

* Do you know of such people like the one above in the reading?

* Do you know of many people like this?

Fable 10   The Fox and Mother Nature

A fox, running from some hunters and dogs, complained to Mother Nature. "How is it that I am always the victim?" he said.

Mother Nature smiled and replied, "Victim? You the victim? Tell that to the squirrels that you have hunted down and eaten. Tell that to the birds whose eggs you have destroyed. And tell that to the moles, frogs, and rats that you have dined on repeatedly."

Moral: *The wicked always see themselves as 'the victims'.*

寓言 10   狐狸和大自然母亲

一只狐狸，一边跑着躲避猎人和狗，一边向大自然母亲抱怨，说："为什么我总是那个受害者？"

大自然母亲微笑着回答说，"受害者？你是受害者吗？告诉那些被你猎杀并吃掉的松鼠吧。告诉那些被你毁掉了鸟蛋的小鸟吧。然后告诉那些你反复吃过无数次的鼹鼠，青蛙和老鼠吧。"

寓意：邪恶的人总是把自己当作受害者。

Taking It a Step Further ——Moral Prompts

* What is your reaction when you see hateful people who claim to be victims? What would you tell them?

* If you were to see someone bullied, how would you personally react?

Fable 11   The Monkey and the Fishermen

A monkey sat in a large tree. He saw some fishermen casting their nets into a river. He closely watched them haul the catch in, take out the fish, and cook them. The monkey saw how happy the men were. So he waited until the men went to sleep.

The monkey snuck up and grabbed the remains of one fish. As he gulped down the fish, several bones got stuck in his throat. This caused him to gag, cough, and jump around in panic. This alerted the fishermen, who caught the monkey and sold it to a zoo.

Moral: *There are reasons why some things are discarded.*

寓言 11　猴子和渔夫

一只猴子坐在一棵大树上。他看到一些渔民把网撒到河里。他密切观察，看到他们拽回渔网，挑拣出鱼，然后开始做饭。猴子看到渔夫们特别高兴，于是等到他们都入睡。

猴子悄悄靠近，抓起了一条鱼的残骸。当他吞下鱼的时侯，几根骨头卡在了他的喉咙里。这导致他非常惊慌地捂着嘴，咳嗽，跳来跳去。它的举动让渔民惊醒。他们抓住了猴子并把它出售给了动物园。

寓意：人们放弃一些东西，是事出有因。

Taking It a Step Further ——Moral Prompts

* Do you have too many things in your life?

* What should you discard?

Fable 12　The Boys, the Frogs, and the Bears

"OK. This is the game. For each frog you hit, you get one point," exclaimed one boy to his friends. "The boy with the most points wins. Do you all have enough stones?"

All the boys nodded. They took various positions along the shore of a lake. Then they began throwing stones at the frogs lying on the rocks or lily pads. The "game" went on for about five minutes. Then the boys overheard the following remark.

OK, the game goes like this. For each kid you get, you get one point. Do you all understand?" The boys slowly turned around. They found themselves staring into the faces of nine large bears.

Moral: *Realize that those who can copy you might become a real threat.*

寓言 12 男孩儿，青蛙和熊

"让我们来做个游戏。打中一只青蛙，就会得一分。" 一个男孩大声对他的朋友们说。"得分最高的男孩儿获胜。你们都有足够的石头吗？"

所有的男孩都点了点头。他们在湖岸边占据了各自的位置，然后就开始向躺在岩石上或是睡莲浮叶上的青蛙扔石头。"游戏" 大概进行了五分钟。然后男孩们听到下面这段话。

"游戏是这样的。每吃掉一个孩子，你就会得到一分。都明白了吗？"男孩们慢慢转过身。他们发现自己正盯着九只大熊的脸。

寓意：必须意识到，那些能够抄袭你的人，可能真正构成威胁。

Taking It a Step Further ——Moral Prompts

* If you were to "copy" something or someone, what would it be? Would it be a composition, a dance, artwork, a song?

* Do you think people who copy someone or something ever become famous? Why or why not?

Fable 13   The Tortoise and the Rabbit

A tortoise was moving slowly along the road. He was almost run over by a rabbit who was running at top speed. The rabbit crashed into a ditch by the road.

The rabbit was very angry and in pain. He began to insult the tortoise. The rabbit shouted, "Creatures like you should be kept in caves!" The tortoise's pride was hurt. He said, "I'm moving as fast as I can. And I have every right to be on the road."

"Oh yeah," replied the rabbit. "You are the slowest creature alive!" The tortoise defended himself. Then he challenged the rabbit to a race.

The two animals soon made arrangements and a course was set. Moles, squirrels, foxes, horses, bats, birds, cows, owls, frogs, and other animals lined up to cheer on the two runners.

The race started. The rabbit was very fast. He left the tortoise behind in a cloud of dust. All the animals cheered on the tortoise. There was no other runner in sight. Because of its slow pace, the tortoise was able to greet all the animals. He could also have a long conversation with each animal along the road. The rabbit won, of course, but it was the tortoise who had dinner with all of his new friends.

Moral: *Winning doesn't guarantee you more friends or fun.*

寓言 13　乌龟和兔子

一只乌龟在路上缓慢地移动。他几乎被一只兔子撞翻，因为兔子在以最快的速度奔跑。兔子撞到了路边的一条沟里。

兔子很生气，也很痛苦。他开始侮辱乌龟。兔子大声喊道："像你这样的生物，应该被养在山洞里！"乌龟的自尊心受到了伤害。他说："我正在尽我所能，努力前进。而且我权利在路上走。"

"哦，是的。"兔子回答，"你是世界上存活的最慢的生物！"乌龟为自己辩护，然后他向兔子发起了挑战。两只动物很快商量好，并确定了比赛路线。鼹鼠，松鼠，狐狸，马，蝙蝠，小鸟，牛，猫头鹰，青蛙和其他动物们都来排队，为两个赛跑者欢呼。

比赛开始了。兔子跑得很快。他把乌龟远远地留在了一片尘土中。于是所有的动物都为乌龟加油，因为他们的视野里已经看不到其他的赛跑者。

由于步伐缓慢，乌龟问候了所有迎接它的动物。他还和路边的每只动物都进行了长时间的交谈。兔子理所当然地赢了，可是乌龟却和他的新朋友们一起共进晚餐。

寓意：赢了比赛并不意味着交到更多的朋友，或是体会到更多的乐趣。

Taking It a Step Further ——Moral Prompts

* Do you think people get too caught up in winning?

* Which is more important: winning or just enjoying the sport ?

Fable 14   The Girls and Their Shadows

A young girl was walking with her friend. They began to compare their shadows on the sidewalk. The younger girl said, "My shadow looks better than yours." The older girl smiled and replied, "But my shadow is much smarter than yours."

The younger girl stopped and thought for a minute. Then she replied, "Hey, they are only shadows. They don't need to be smart. Just good-looking."

Moral: *The shadows we cast are not a true reflection of ourselves.*

寓言 14　女孩们和影子

一个小女孩正在朋友们散步。她们开始比较人行道上的影子。小女孩说："我的影子比你们的影子都好看。" 大一些的女孩笑着，回答说："但是我的影子比你的更聪明。"

小女孩停下来，想了一会儿，然后她回答说："嘿，它们都只是阴影。他们不需要聪明。好看就可以。"

寓意：我们投下的影子并不能真实地反映我们自己。

Taking It a Step Further ——Moral Prompts

* How do people generally see you, just as good-looking or smart or funny?

* If you were to change your image, what would you focus on?

Fable 15　The Mouse and the Bull

A bull was to be sold to a slaughterhouse. He complained bitterly about his fate. But he was tied up. So there was no escape. A mouse spoke up and said, "Perhaps I can help."

The bull mocked him, "How could such a little thing like you help me? I'm a hundred times larger and stronger than you."

The mouse didn't reply. It simply went up and gnawed the rope that tied the bull. It wasn't long before the bull was free. "I was wrong, little one," said the bull. "Sometimes, the little can be more useful than the large and strong."

Moral: *Usefulness comes in all sizes.*

寓言 15　老鼠和公牛

一头公牛将被卖到屠宰场。他痛苦地抱怨自己的命运。但是他被绑起来了，已经不能逃脱了。一只老鼠对它说，"也许我能帮你。"

公牛嘲笑它说，"像你这样的小东西，怎么能帮到我？我比你强大一百倍。"

老鼠没有回答。它只是爬上去，啃咬绑住了公牛的绳子。很快，公牛就恢复了自由。"我错了，小家伙，"公牛说。"有时候，小人物比强大的人更能发挥作用。"

寓意：天生我才必有用。

Taking It a Step Further ——Moral Prompts

* Are you influenced by someone's height?

* Do you feel shorter people, even dwarfs, are not fully respected?

Fable 16   The Woman and Her Children

A poor laundry woman had two children. She wanted her children to grow up intelligent. She worked long hours to pay for school supplies and tutors.

Her children learned that when they wanted more paper, their mother bought it without question. They also learned that when they asked for more pencils and books, they always got them. The children then decided to ask for better clothes. "Mother," they said, "we can't just be intelligent. We also have to look intelligent."

The mother worked hard to get this money, and soon the new clothes were handed over. The children next decided that they needed better food. "Intelligence, dear mother, needs to be fed well. It is not enough to be intelligent. You have to show this intelligence in your body. A skinny body is a sign of no intelligence," they exclaimed. Their mother then gave them better food. The children then decided that they needed dessert. They exclaimed that intelligence needs sugary sweets. But their mother replied, "That's it! I decided that I simply cannot afford intelligent children anymore. I will just have hard-working children. So, out you both go to do laundry."

Moral: *Intelligence is nothing without hard work.*

寓言 16　女人和她的孩子们

一个可怜的洗衣妇有两个孩子。她希望孩子们能够成长为聪明的人。她花很长时间工作，来支付学校用品的费用和老师的补习费。

她的孩子们知道，当他们想要更多的纸张时，妈妈会毫不犹豫地去买。他们还知道，当他们要更多的铅笔和书时，也会得到。然后，孩子们决定要更好的衣服。他们说："妈妈，我们不能只是变得聪明。还应该看起来聪明。"

母亲为了获得买衣服的钱努力工作，很快就把新衣服买给了孩子们。接下来，孩子们决定他们需要更好的食物。"亲爱的妈妈，聪明需要有吃的食物来滋养。仅仅变聪明是远远不够的。我们还需要通过身体来表现我们的聪明。瘦弱的身体是没有智商的表现。"他们大声说。接着，妈妈就给了他们更好的食物。然后，孩子们决定他们需要甜点。他们大声疾呼，聪明需要含糖的零食。但是，他们的母亲回答说："就是这样！我意识到，我再也负担不起聪明的孩子的需求。我只想要努力勤奋的孩子。所以，你们俩个都出去洗衣服吧。"

寓意：不努力的话，聪明等于一无所有。

Taking It a Step Further——Moral Prompts

* Do you consider yourself intelligent and hardworking? Why?

* Do you feel that hardworking people succeed more in life than just

  hardworking ones? Or vice versa?

Fable 17　The Two Frogs

Two frogs were neighbors. One lived in a deep pond and one lived under an old wooden house. The frog that lived in the pond went to visit his friend near the house. "How can you live here?" remarked the frog. "It's positively noisy, and dangerous. Maybe those giants will find you and eat you," the pond frog added.

The house frog merely replied that it seemed safe, and there was probably no danger. But he said that it would nice to visit the frog's pond.

Upon seeing the pond, the house frog said, "Oh my, it's positively noisy, and very dangerous. Look at those cranes. Why, they are eating machines, every frog knows that! And look at those alligators!"

The pond frog merely replied that it seemed safe and that he had never been harmed. The house frog could only reply, "It seems that we are both deaf and blind then!"

Moral: *Familiarity quiets the noise and minimizes the danger.*

寓言 17　两只青蛙

两只青蛙彼此是邻居。一只住在一个深深的池塘里，另一只住在一所老木屋。住在池塘里的那只青蛙去看望它家附近的朋友。"你怎么住在这儿？"这只青蛙说。"这简直太吵了，而且很危险。那些巨人们可能会找到你，并把你吃掉。"住在池塘里的青蛙又补充说。

住在房子里的青蛙只是回答说，这儿看起来很安全，好像没什么危险。但是它说，如果能参观好朋友的池塘，那真是太好了。

看到池塘后，住在房子里的青蛙说："哦，天哪，这简直太吵了，而且很危险。看看那些起重机。天啊，他们在吃机器！所有青蛙都知道的！再看看那些鳄鱼！"

住在池塘里的青蛙只是回答说，这儿好像很安全，而且它从未受到过伤害。住在房子里的青蛙只能可以回答说："看起来我们两个都是又聋又瞎！"

寓意：对环境的熟悉可以减少噪音感，并且把危险降低到最小。

Taking It a Step Further -- Moral Prompts

* Do you think that familiarity makes you unaware of various dangers or more aware of the dangers around you?

* What kinds of environments are you not so familiar with?

Fable 18   The Seller of Super Heroes

A merchant made various plastic toy figures of super heroes and amusement park mascots. One day, some school children were walking home past his stall. He yelled out, "Look at these wonderful super heroes. If you buy now, they will protect you." The children crowded around for a better look.

"How can these things protect us?" asked one girl. The seller was surprised. "Huh, well... he will be close and can protect you, see."

"But how?" asked a boy. "It's just plastic." The seller backed away, and then said, "Well, yes, it's plastic, but there is magic in the belief."

"But what if we don't believe that the super hero can protect us?" asked another girl. This led to more and more questions until the man packed up his figures and closed his stall.

Moral: *Protection rarely comes in plastic.*

寓言18 卖超级英雄的小贩

一位商人制作了各种塑料玩具，包括超级英雄的玩偶和游乐园的吉祥物。有一天，一些小学生在回家的路上，经过了他的摊位。他大声喊："快看这些了不起的超级英雄！如果你现在买，它们马上就会保护你。" 孩子们围拢过来，想仔细看看。

"这些东西如何保护我们？" 一个女孩问。小贩很惊讶。"嗯，是这样……瞧，他会很亲密地保护你。"

"但是怎样保护我呢？" 一个男孩问。"它只是塑料。" 小贩向后退了一步，然后说："嗯，是的，它们是塑料的，但是信念会充满魔法。"

"但是，如果我们不相信超级英雄能保护我们，怎么办？" 另一个女孩问。这引起了越来越多的疑问。那个小贩只好收拾自己的玩偶，关闭了摊位。

寓意：塑料（这样脆弱的材料）几乎不能提供任何保护。

Taking It a Step Further ——Moral Prompts

* Do you consider yourself superstitious? Do you have any "lucky charms?"

* Are superheroes a childish concept or do they serve a real purpose in society?

Fable 19 The Woodcutter and the Pig

Deep in a forest, a woodcutter was relaxing from cutting firewood. A large black pig waddled by, snorting and digging in the soil for acorns. Puzzled by the man, the pig stopped and sniffed.

Then the pig asked, "Can I be of any help? Or do you need an acorn?"

The man smiled and said that he was content. The pig replied, "Humph! Content? How can you be content? You have no acorns!" The woodcutter could only say, "But I don't need acorns. I am happy with what I have."

The pig snorted, "Sounds like foolishness to me. Real happiness has to be earned! You have to work for it! Look at me, I must have 2000 acorns, and I am just beginning." With that the pig began digging around the man's feet, soon coming up with an acorn. "Hah, see, another one! 2001 acorns! THIS is happiness." The man took the acorn and looked at it carefully. Then he said, "No, this is only an acorn. Your happiness is only in your imagination. And....oh yes....my happiness doesn't have me digging around in the dirt either." With that, the woodcutter threw the acorn far away. The pig squealed in horror at losing it.

Moral: *You will be possessed by your possessions if you cannot find happiness within yourself.*

寓言 19　樵夫和猪

在森林深处，一名樵夫砍了一些柴火，正在放松休息。一只大黑猪蹒跚着走过来，鼻子一边发出哼哼的声音，一边在土里拱来拱去，寻找橡子。看到樵夫，猪很疑惑，于是停下来，抽着鼻子。

接着，猪问樵夫："我能帮上什么忙吗？你需要橡子吗？"

樵夫笑着说，他非常满足。猪回答说："哼！满足？你怎么能满足？你没有橡子！"樵夫只能回答说："但是我不需要橡子。我对自己的所有非常满意。"

猪哼了一声，"对我来说，这真是愚蠢的想法。真正的幸福必须通过努力获得！你必须为之奋斗！看着我，我已经拥有 2000 颗橡子，而这才是刚刚开始。"

于是，猪开始在樵夫的脚边拱来拱去，很快就找到了一颗橡子。"哈哈，快看！第 2001 颗橡子！这就是幸福。"男人拿起橡子，仔细地看了看。然后他说："不，这只是颗橡子。你的幸福只有在你的想象里。而且....哦，是的....在我的幸福里，我也不用在泥土里四处乱挖，拱来拱去。"说完这些，樵夫把橡子扔出去很远。猪因为失去了橡子，惊恐地尖叫。

寓意：如果你不能找到内在的幸福，你就会被你所拥有的东西左右。

* Do you think material objects and products are needed to make one happy?

* Do you know many people who have "nothing" but are very happy?

Fable 20   Labor Disputes

One day a farmer named Dohama was plowing his fields. His cow turned to him, exhausted, and said, "Sorry, Dohama, I can't go any further. I'm too thirsty."

"THIRSTY?" shouted back Dohama. "Well, join the club! I'm just a poor farmer and water is expensive."

"Well, if you really appreciated me," continued the cow, "you would give me water. I do more for you than all of your friends. Your friends just give you pleasure. I help you to grow your crops."

"Huh? Well......you don't have to bring my friends into this! Well......OK! OK!" mumbled Dohama.

As he got the water from his fish pond, the fish raced to him to complain. "We are tired of this small pond. We need a much bigger pond!"

"A BIGGER pond! Do you all realize how long it would take to make a bigger pond?" exclaimed Dohama. His fish ignored this question and only replied, "If you really valued us, you would want us to be happy. After all, we help to feed your family."

Dohama thought and thought. "Happy fish? Well, I suppose this is important! OK, OK! I will make your pond bigger," he replied.

As he entered his barn to get a shovel to make the pond larger, his chickens flew down to him. "Dohama! Your house cat keeps chasing us! It's crazy. How can you expect us to lay eggs, if we don't feel safe?"

"Well, cats do this. It's only natural," replied Dohama. "If you really treasured us," the chickens said, "you would tie that cat. After all, we—"

"I KNOW, I KNOW," replied Dohama. So all that day Dohama managed to fix a variety of problems, all of which pleased his animals. And later that year, Dohama, in turn, was the richest man in the area. He had the best crops, and the most fish and eggs of any farmer. All because of his devoted animals.

Moral: *One must give respect to have respect.*

寓言20 劳动纠纷

一天，一位名叫多哈马（Dohama）的农夫正在耕田。他的牛精疲力尽，转过身对他说道："对不起，多哈马，我再也走不动了。我太渴了。"

"渴？"多哈马大声回答说。"好吧，你应该加入一个（供水）俱乐部！我只是一个贫穷的农夫，水很贵的。"

"可是，如果你真正欣赏我的话，" 母牛接着说，"你会给我水喝。和你所有的朋友比，我为你做的比他们都多。你的朋友仅仅给你带来快乐。我帮你种庄稼。"

"嗯？好吧 ... 你不用把我的朋友也代入这个问题！行吧 ...· 好的！好的！"多哈马嘟囔着。

当他从鱼塘里取水时，鱼纷纷向他抱怨。"我们都厌倦了这个小池塘。我们需要一个更大的池塘！"

"更大的池塘！你们知道，建造一个更大的池塘需要多长时间吗？"多哈马大叫。他的鱼都无视这个问题，只是回答说："如果你真正珍惜我们，你会希望我们幸福。毕竟，我们帮助你养家糊口。"

多哈马想了想。"幸福的鱼？好吧，我假设这很重要！好的，好的！我会把你们的池塘变大。"他回答说。

当他进入谷仓去拿锹想扩建池塘的时候，他的鸡都飞了下来。"多哈马！你家的猫一直在追我们！它很疯狂。如果我们感到不安全，你怎么指望我们下蛋？"

"好吧，猫确实是这样。这是很自然的事情。"多哈马回答说。"如果你确实认为我们有价值，"小鸡们说，"那你会把那只猫绑起来。毕竟，我们。。。"

"我知道，我知道。"多哈马回答。于是，那一整天，为了取悦他的动物们，多哈马设法解决了各种问题。那一年的晚些时候，多哈马顺理成章地成了他所在地区的首富。在所有农夫里，他的庄稼收成最好，拥有最多的鱼和鸡蛋。这些都是因为他对动物们的献身服务。

寓意：首先要尊重别人才能获得尊重。

Taking It a Step Further -- Moral Prompts

* Do you think older people show you a lot of respect?

* Do you show older people a lot of respect? To whom do you not
  respect and why?

Fable 21   The Debut

"Of course, they took a very long time to make," boasted a butterfly named Jigil on one hot day in June. "See the different shades of brown and the various patterns!" The crowd of spiders, grasshoppers, and ants all soon began to gasp in wonder.

"See how clear the lines are too. My wings are the most beautiful in the entire world. Come CLOSER, come CLOSER, dear friends," Jigil added.

Indeed, Jigil's admirers did come closer. They touched, smelled, measured, and praised the texture, colors, and thickness of Jigil's new wings. As the day continued, Jigil added boast after boast.

He finally said, "Friends, I must be leaving. You will now see my wonderful wings carry me far away." Jigil ran and jumped into the air.

But instead of sailing into the wind, he crashed a few feet away. He looked back at his useless wings. They were smeared, torn, and cut from so much admiration.

Moral: *Modesty will lift you higher than any boast.*

寓言 21　首次亮相

"当然，他们需要很长时间才能长出来。" 在六月的一个炎热日子，一只名叫吉吉尔的蝴蝶在吹嘘自己。"看见这些不同色调的棕色和各种图案了吧！" 很快，蜘蛛，蚱蜢和蚂蚁开始惊叹不已。

"看这些线条多么清晰。我的翅膀是全世界最美丽的。靠近点，再靠近点，亲爱的朋友们。" 吉吉尔补充说。

的确，吉吉尔的仰慕者们都走近他。他们抚摸，用鼻子闻，丈量着尺寸，赞扬吉吉尔的新翅膀的质地，颜色和厚度。一天的时间过去了，吉吉尔一次又一次地夸耀自己。

最后他说："朋友们，我必须走了。您现在马上会看到，我的美丽翅膀将把我带到远方。" 吉吉尔奔跑着跳向空中。

但是他没有能在风中翱翔，而是跌在了几英尺远的地方。他回头看了着没用的翅膀。因为太多的仰慕，它们已经沾满了油污，还有撕裂和伤口。

寓意：和炫耀相比，谦虚会把你举得更高。

Taking It a Step Further -- Moral Prompts

* Do you know of any braggards? How do you react to their bragging?

* Do you know of any modest people? Are you really modest?

Fable 22   The Ugly Slug

"I'm so ugly," said a slug to a butterfly, after seeing itself in a puddle. "Perhaps you could use some whitening lotion and wrinkle cream. And maybe some blush under your antennas," said the butterfly.

"Oh, is that all? Will I then be perfect? Will I be like you?" said the slug.

"No, no, no, my little one!" laughed the butterfly. "It is not so easy." The butterfly then ordered the slug to try mud masks, mascara, oil control treatments, and mists. The slug looked very different under many layers of cosmetics. It asked, "Am I now perfect? Am I now like you?"

Before the butterfly could answer, a bluebird, attracted by the shiny colors, flew down and ate the slug.

Moral: *Perfection brings problems.*

寓言 22　丑陋的鼻涕虫

"我好丑"，在水坑里看到自己的容貌，一只鼻涕虫对蝴蝶说。"或许你可以用一些美白乳液和抗皱霜。也可以在你的触须下面用一些腮红。" 蝴蝶说。

"哦，就这些吗？那我会变得完美吗？我会像你一样吗？" 鼻涕虫说。

"不，不，不，我的小家伙！" 蝴蝶笑了。"可没那么容易。" 接着，蝴蝶又命令鼻涕虫试一试黑泥面膜，睫毛膏，控油水和喷雾式补水液。用了许多层化妆品，鼻涕虫看起来确实很不一样。它问："我现在完美了吗？我现在像你一样吗？"

在蝴蝶回答之前，一只蓝鸲被闪亮的各种颜色吸引，飞下来吃掉了鼻涕虫。

寓意：完美会带来麻烦。

Taking It a Step Further ——Moral Prompts

* Are you under pressure to have perfect grades and to look perfect?

* Do you know of any perfectionists in your own life? Are they
  happy?

Fable 23   Over There…

A flock of sheep lost their shepherd and guard dog. They elected a leader to take them to better pastures and then back home. Some sheep advised their new leader to go to through the forest. But as they came near the forest, the noise and darkness scared the younger sheep. They insisted that their leader take them around the forest and across the mountain.

"Of course," the sheep leader said. "There's nothing more important than safety." They began to go up the mountain. However, the older sheep complained, "It's too hard to climb the trail. And it's too cold."

"Yes, yes, easier is better," the leader replied. Soon most of the flock thought that home must be just over the hills. This led to even more suggestions, all of which the leader agreed to. And so, for the next week, the flock of sheep traveled through several valleys, hills, and forests. But they only ended up in the same pasture where they had started.

Moral: *Real leaders are not led by their followers.*

寓言 23　在那儿

一群绵羊失去了他们的牧羊人和牧羊犬。他们选出了一位领头羊，带他们去更好的牧场，然后回家。一些绵羊劝说他们的新领袖带他们穿越树林。但是当他们走到树林附近时，喧嚣和黑暗把小羊们吓坏了。他们坚持认为，他们的领导应该带他们绕过树林，穿越山脉。

"当然，" 领头的绵羊说。"没有什么比安全更重要。"他们开始上山。可是，年长的绵羊们抱怨说："爬这条小路太艰难了。而且还这么冷。"

"是的，是的，越轻松越好。" 领导的绵羊回答。很快，大多数绵羊都认为翻过了小山，就是他们的家。这又引来了更多的建议，而领头羊对所有的建议都表示赞同。于是，在接下来的一周里，这群绵羊穿越了几个山谷、小山和树林。

但是他们最终又回到了他们出发的那个牧场。

寓意：真正的领导人不会受部下的左右。

Taking It a Step Further ——Moral Prompts

* What do you think of most world leaders?

* Do you think most world leaders listen to their own "people" or do they mostly ignore them?

Volume 5

Fable 1 The Silkworms and Their Owner

A maker of silk in China noticed that his black 'silkworm' caterpillars were taking their time to make a cocoon, from which he could make his silk. He asked them what the problem was, and they said, "We hear rumors that after we spin our wonderful silk cocoon, you will just kill us just before we emerge. Then you use the cocoon for your strange purposes."

"Well, some of this is true," coughed the owner, "but I glorify you by making your cocoons into the most wonderful of all cloths, and have people rave about your silk. Nothing could be better than this."

"Yes, living our lives could be better than this 'glory,' and so, we are NOT going to make any cocoons for you."

Moral: *The promise of glory doesn't always produce loyalty.*

寓言 1　蚕蛹和他们的主人

一位中国的丝绸制造商注意到，他的黑色蚕蛹们需要很长时间结茧，而他需要这些蚕茧来制作丝绸。于是他问蚕蛹们出了什么问题。他们说：“我们听到了谣言。在我们结成美妙的蚕茧后，你会在我们被孵化之前杀死我们。蚕茧会被用来达到你的可疑目的。”

“嗯，这话有些是真的，”主人咳嗽了一下，说，“但我把你的茧做成了所有布料中最漂亮的，让人们对你们的丝赞不绝口。没有比这更好的了。”

“是的，我们能够活着可能比这种‘荣耀’更好。所以，我们不会再为你生产任何蚕茧。”

寓意：　有关荣耀的许诺并不能保证忠诚。

Taking It a Step Further ——Moral Prompts

* What issue would cause you to be more loyal to someone?

* Is the idea of being more famous and having glory appealing to you?

Fable 2　The Great Debate

A dog came across a frog as it was sniffing its way through a forest. As the dog had never seen a frog before, the dog said, “My, you are the ugliest creature I have EVER seen.”

The frog was insulted and blurted out, “And you are the ugliest creature that I have EVER seen.”

An owl, which had been watching the interaction, mumbled, "You both are the ugliest creatures that I have EVER seen." The two protested and chorused that, without a doubt, the owl was the ugliest creature ever to exist. It wasn't long that the three called together a panel of animals to decide if they were indeed ugly AND which one was the best looking. Bats, moles, birds, rats, squirrels, beavers, deer, pigs, otters, lynx, anteaters, foxes, bears, and one panther soon debated the issue.

After a long and loud debate, they decided that the frog, dog, and owls were all equally ugly and that none could even be called good-looking. At this time, the panther, who had remained strangely silent the entire time, sauntered slowly up to the three, eyeing them with wonder, before saying, "You all might be ugly, but you all look extremely tasty."

And with that, he pounced on three of them and had them for lunch.

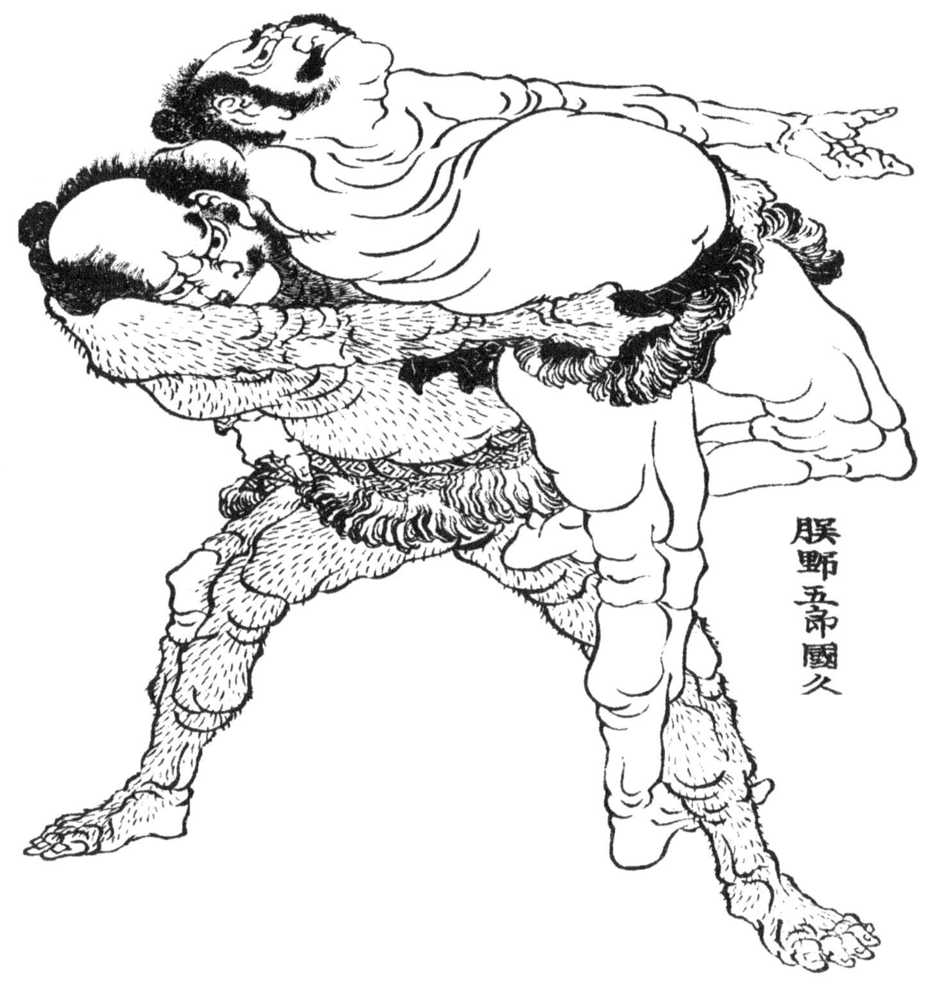

Moral: Perceptions of beauty are always in the eye of the beholder.

*Sometimes, it is not beauty that catches the eye.

寓言2　伟大的辩论

狗在森林里嗅探着赶路，他遇到了一只青蛙。因为狗从未见过青蛙，于是他说："天哪，你是我见过的最丑的生物。"

青蛙受了侮辱，脱口而出："你才是我见过的最丑的生物。"

一只猫头鹰一直在观看狗和青蛙的互动。他嘟囔着说："你们都是我见过的最丑的生物。"狗和青蛙齐声抗议说，毫无疑问，猫头鹰才是有史以来最丑陋的生物。很快，狗，青蛙和猫头鹰召集了一群动物来决定他们是否真地很丑，哪一位长得最好看。蝙蝠、鼹鼠、小鸟、老鼠、松鼠、海狸、鹿、猪、水獭、猞猁、食蚁兽、狐狸、熊和黑豹很快就这个问题展开了辩论。

经过长时间的激烈辩论，他们一致认为青蛙，狗，猫头鹰同样丑陋，甚至没有誰能被称为好看。就在这个时候，一直诡异地保持沉默的黑豹缓缓地走到了他们三个跟前，疑惑地看着他们，说道："你们可能长得都很丑，但是你们看起来都很美味。"说完，他扑向了他们仨，把他们当成了午餐。

寓意：　　旁观者能更好地洞察美貌。

　　　　　*有时，惹人注意的不是一个人的美貌。

Taking It a Step Further ——Moral Prompts

* Do you think that beauty is in the eye of the 'beholder'?

* How would you describe a beautiful woman or handsome man?

Fable 3 Is It Safe?

A salamander and a lizard saw two boys who were out in the forest. They were throwing rocks and hitting bushes and trees with their bats, and so the two creatures decided to hide up in a tree.

"WHY are these humans doing so much destruction?" bemoaned the lizard.

The salamander eyed the lizard and guessed that the humans were sent by the gods to punish the lizards for their bad behavior. The lizard protested and retorted that 'no, in fact, humans were created by the sun to punish the salamanders for their bad behavior.' After some time, the noise from the boys seemed to grow quiet, and it seemed as if the boys had simply gone away.

"Let's say, 'you're right'" whispered the salamander, "and these humans were sent by the sun to punish us. In this situation, you wouldn't be harmed, now would you? Why don't you climb down and see if it's safe?"

The lizard was startled but could find no way to reply, and so it began to slowly edge its way down the tree, all the while muttering to itself, "What do I know about the sun and punishments? I should have kept my mouth shut!"

Moral: Accusations should always be made with great care.

寓言 3　安全吗？

蝾螈和蜥蜴看到了两个男孩在森林里。他们扔着石头，用球棒击打着灌木和树。蝾螈和蜥蜴这两个家伙决定躲在一棵树里。

"为什么这些人类要进行如此大规模的破坏？"蜥蜴哀叹道。

蝾螈看着蜥蜴，猜想说人类是上帝派来的，以他们的不良行为来惩罚蜥蜴。蜥蜴抗议并反驳说，"不，实际上，人类是由太阳创造的，以他们的不良行为来惩罚蝾螈。"

过了一会儿，男孩子们的喧闹声似乎渐渐安静了下来，好像他们已经离开了一样。

"好吧，'你是对的'，"蝾螈低声嘟囔着，"这些人类是被太阳派来惩罚我们的。现在这样的状况，你不会受到伤害，是吧？你为什么不爬下去看看是否安全？"

蜥蜴吓了一跳，却不知道该怎样回答。于是它一边开始慢慢地沿着树干朝下蠕动，一边喃喃自语："我又怎么知道太阳和惩罚的意思？我就是应该闭嘴！"

寓意： 指责别人的时候要万分小心。

Taking It a Step Further ——Moral Prompts

* Have you ever been accused of something?

* Do you know of people who make a lot of careless accusations?

What is the best way of dealing with such people

Fable 4　The Two Boat Men

Two oarsmen were rowing down a mighty river in China and were thrown this way and that by the current. It was slowly going,　which caused the two men to start to argue.

"If we hang on the left bank, we will get to our destination faster." His companion disputed the claim and said that there were just too many sandbars that could wreck the boat to risk it.

"Well," the first boatman then said, "We should go straight down the middle then, maybe that's better."

"Yeah, that might be better, but I know nothing about the middle. But if going to the left bank is too dangerous. The right bank gives us nothing but grief with these crazy currents. Let's go to the middle then!"

And so the two men steered the boat straight into the middle of the river. This, however, led them straight into a giant whirlpool that destroyed the vessel and almost drowned the two men.

Moral: Agreement with one's ideas does not necessarily signal progress.

寓言 4　两个船夫

　　两个划桨手在中国的一条巨大的河流上划船。船被水流抛来抛去，行驶得很缓慢，于是两个人争吵起来。

　　"如果我们一直沿着岸的左边前进，我们会更快到达目的地。"他的同伴对这一看法提出异议，说沙洲太多，可能损坏船体，所以不能冒险。

　　"嗯，" 第一个船夫说，"那我们就一直在河的中间往前走，这样可能更好。"

　　"是的，那样可能更好。但我对河床中间的部分一无所知。可是如果沿着岸的左边行进实在太危险了。岸的右边那些疯狂的水流只给我们带来悲伤。那我们就在河中央前进吧！"

　　就这样，两个人把船直接开到了河中央。然而，这导致他们直接进入了一个巨大的漩涡，船只被摧毁，两个人也几乎溺水。

寓意：同意别人的想法并不一定意味着进步。

Taking It a Step Further ——Moral Prompts

* Have you ever been pressured to agree to do something?

* Do you think the idea of harmony and agreement is stressed too
　　much in your society or not enough?

Fable 5 The Invitation

A corn snake was hungry and decided that it was time to dine on some rats. But the snake was vexed as to exactly how to get some rats even close to its hole. The snake slithered around pondering this question, and eventually, it sent a bouquet of flowers to the rat mound on the nearby hill.

Along with it, the snake wrote: "My dear esteemed, neighbors, I am herewith asking to invite you to dinner. I have been puzzled over the issue of 'the chicken or the egg.' Yes, which came first? This question has become a huge issue with us snakes, and it might lead to a war. So, we need impartial and wise creatures like you to decide on this issue. So, please come around seven, won't you?"

Upon receiving the flowers and invitation, the rats discussed it at length. The young rats were quite eager to have a free dinner, until one old rat pointed out, "The issue is not the chicken or egg, it is 'what is for dinner'. And the answer is that 'we are'. Chicken or egg! REALLY?"

"But this dispute may cause a war," chorused out the young rats.

"GOOD! Let the snakes go to war then. It will just make our lives better, and if they are stupid enough to go to war over a silly puzzle, then they need to kill each other off."

Moral: Strange invitations are always a sign of trouble.

寓言 5 邀请

　　一条玉米蛇饿感觉到了饥饿。它决定是时候该吃一些老鼠了。但是这条蛇非常烦恼，不知道如何让老鼠靠近它的洞穴。蛇盘旋着思索着这个问题，最终，它送了一束鲜花到附近山上的鼠丘。

　　和鲜花一起送去的还有邀请。蛇写道："我亲爱的尊敬的邻居们，我在此特意邀请您共进晚餐。我一直对"先有鸡还是先有蛋"的问题感到困惑。是的，哪个先出现呢？这个问题已经成为我们蛇族的一个大难题，它可能会导致一场战争。所以，我们需要像您这样公正而睿智的人来决定这个问题。所以，请七点左右过来，好吗？"

　　收到鲜花和邀请后，老鼠们进行了长时间的讨论。年轻的老鼠们非常渴望有一顿免费的晚餐，直到一只上了年纪的老鼠指出，"这个问题并不是先有鸡还是先有蛋，而是'晚餐吃什么'，而答案就是'我们'。先有鸡还是先有蛋！真是这样吗？"

　　"但这场争端可能会引发战争，"年轻的老鼠们齐声喊道。

　　"很好！那就让蛇都去打仗吧。那样的话，我们的生活会变得更美好，如果他们愚蠢至极，为了一个无聊的谜题而开战，那么就让他们自相残杀吧。"

寓意： 莫名其妙的邀请总是会带来麻烦。

Taking It a Step Further ——Moral Prompts

* Have you ever refused an invitation, if so why?

* What are some indications that there might be 'trouble ahead' with

 a particular future interaction?

Fable 6　The Beaver, the Kite, and the Vine

Upon seeing his damn broken by the river and wind, a beaver, raged at the stars, thinking that they were laughing at his plight. The kite likewise, who was blown off-course, and upon seeing the beaver swear at the stars, joined in.

A long vine, which had witnessed both animals acting in such a strange way, called out, "What is the problem? Does not the wind make you stronger? Does not the water make you refreshed? And why do you blame the stars, which are completely oblivious to your sufferings?"

The beaver and the kite slowly turned and looked at the vine, and began to mock it mercilessly. "YOU, a PLANT have the nerve to chastise us? We are ANIMALS, which have to struggle to make our way here, while you have it easy! And you DARE LECTURE US?"

The vine laughed and replied, "You animals claim to be so smart, but you are both so blind. The wind and rain are TEACHING you, don't you see?"

Moral: Problems can be your teachers if you open your eyes.

寓言 6 海狸，风筝和藤蔓

一只海狸看到自己被河水和风弄得身上到处是伤，于是对着星星怒吼，以为它们在嘲笑自己的困境。同样，风筝也被风吹得摇摇欲坠。当它看到海狸对着星星们诅咒，也加入了进来。

一条长长的藤蔓目睹了这两只动物的诡异举动，开口说道："出了什么问题？风不是让你们更强壮吗？水不是会让你们精神焕发吗？你们为什么要责怪那些星星呢？它们根本不在意你们的痛苦。"

海狸和风筝慢慢转过身来，看着藤蔓，开始无情地嘲笑它。"你，就是一棵植物，居然还敢指责我们？我们是动物，它们必须努力奋斗才能在这儿生存，而你却活得很轻松！你还敢教训我们吗？"

藤蔓笑着说："你们这些动物自作聪明，其实你们都是瞎子。风和雨已经给了你们教训，没有看到吗？"

寓意：如果睁开双眼，你会发现存在的问题可以教会你很多东西。

Taking It a Step Further ——Moral Prompts

* Do you think that problems are you teachers?

* What are some lessons you have learned from bad experiences?

Fable 7 The Bobcat and the Crane

A bobcat was stalking a crane at the edge of a lake, and just as he was about to pounce, a frog croaked out 'danger,' and the crane turned, and flew away, just in the nick of time.

The bobcat was incensed! And then started to splatter the water to kill the frog, and all of the frogs if need be, to teach them a lesson. The frogs, however, scattered just as soon as the crane took off, and so the bobcat just got himself incredibly wet.

The bobcat, which now was shivering from the cold, stalked back to dry ground and laid down. It was of two minds, one to wait until the frogs came back and to splatter as many as possible. But there was also the bobcat's hunger, which told him to move on to an 'easier dinner.'

The crane, which was now a safe distance away, said to some other birds, "My! That is ONE stupid animal. The bobcat can't move because of its anger. It will sit there for a very long time, thinking how to teach the frogs 'a lesson'. And the frogs have completely forgotten about me!"

Moral: Revenge can easily become pointless.

寓言 7　山猫和仙鹤

一只山猫在湖边追着一只仙鹤。当他要扑过去的时候，一只青蛙呱呱叫了一声"危险"，于是千钧一发之际，仙鹤转身飞走了。

山猫被激怒了！开始泼水想杀死青蛙，如果需要的话，甚至是所有的青蛙，从而给它们一个教训。可是，当仙鹤一起飞，青蛙们立刻四下散开了，所以山猫只是把自己弄得全身湿漉漉。

山猫因为寒冷而瑟瑟发抖，于是它大步走回到干爽的地面躺下。它有两个想法，一个是等着青蛙们回来，然后尽可能多地泼水。但同时山猫也感到饥饿，这让他想到去享受"更轻松的晚餐"。

仙鹤现在已经和山猫保持安全的距离。它对其他一些鸟说："我的天啊！那真是一种愚蠢的动物。山猫因为愤怒而无法移动。它将会在那儿坐很长时间，思考着如何给青蛙一个教训。青蛙们已经完全把我忘记了！"

寓意：报复很容易变得毫无意义。

Taking It a Step Further ——Moral Prompts

* What is the difference between seeking justice and seeking revenge?

* Have you ever been so angry that you wanted to seek 'revenge' on someone?

Fable 8   The Hyena and the Buffalo

A hyena and a buffalo, which had been captured and put in a zoo, gaped at each other. Both animals had never seen another of its kind before, and could not quite understand the animal that stood before it.

The zookeepers, who were knocking off for the day, said amongst themselves, "Well, they will soon get acquainted and become friends. I mean, what ELSE is there to DO here?" As the people left, and the sky became slowly dark, the two animals squared off. While the hyena began to look at how to make the buffalo dinner, the buffalo slowly pondered how to stomp the hyena into the ground.

As the two sprang and charged each other, they soon found themselves exhausted and no closer to their goals.

"This is STUPID," proclaimed the buffalo. "This is WHAT they, the humans, want US to do. To kill us! We should stop this!"

The hyena laughed, as it cannot do anything else in responding to any creature. "WELL, do you have a BETTER idea, Mr. Buffalo?"

"Well, no I don't!" replied the buffalo. The hyena laughed again, "You are making me extremely nervous about our lack of options." And with that the hyena just darted away, getting as far away from the buffalo as it could.

Moral: Running away may be the best option at certain times.

寓言 8 鬣狗和水牛

一只鬣狗和一头水牛被捕获。它们被圈养在动物园里，彼此目瞪口呆地互相注视着。两只动物以前从未见过另一只同样的异类，也不能完全理解站在面前的动物到底是什么。动物园的管理员们当天要休息。他们互相安慰说："很好。它们很快就会熟悉并成为朋友。我的意思是，在这里还有什么别的事情可以做吗？"

随着人们的离开，天色渐渐暗了下来，两只动物摆好架势，对峙起来。鬣狗开始研究如何才能把水牛当成晚餐，水牛则在慢慢思考如何将鬣狗踩在脚下。

它们一跃而起，冲向对方。可是很快就发现自己已经筋疲力尽，可是距离目标还很远。

"这太愚蠢了，"水牛宣称。"这就是他们--人类，希望我们做的事情。他们要杀了我们！我们应该停止互相攻击！"

鬣狗笑了，因为它意识到自己无能为力去回应别人。"好吧，水牛先生，你有更好的主意吗，？"

"嗯，不，我没有！"水牛回答。

鬣狗又笑了起来，"你让我极度地紧张，因为我们别无选择。"说完，鬣狗就飞奔而去，尽可能地远离水牛。

寓意：有些时候逃跑可能是最好的选择。

Taking It a Step Further ——Moral Prompts

* Have you ever run away from a difficult or dangerous situation?

* What kinds of situations are just 'best' to run away from?

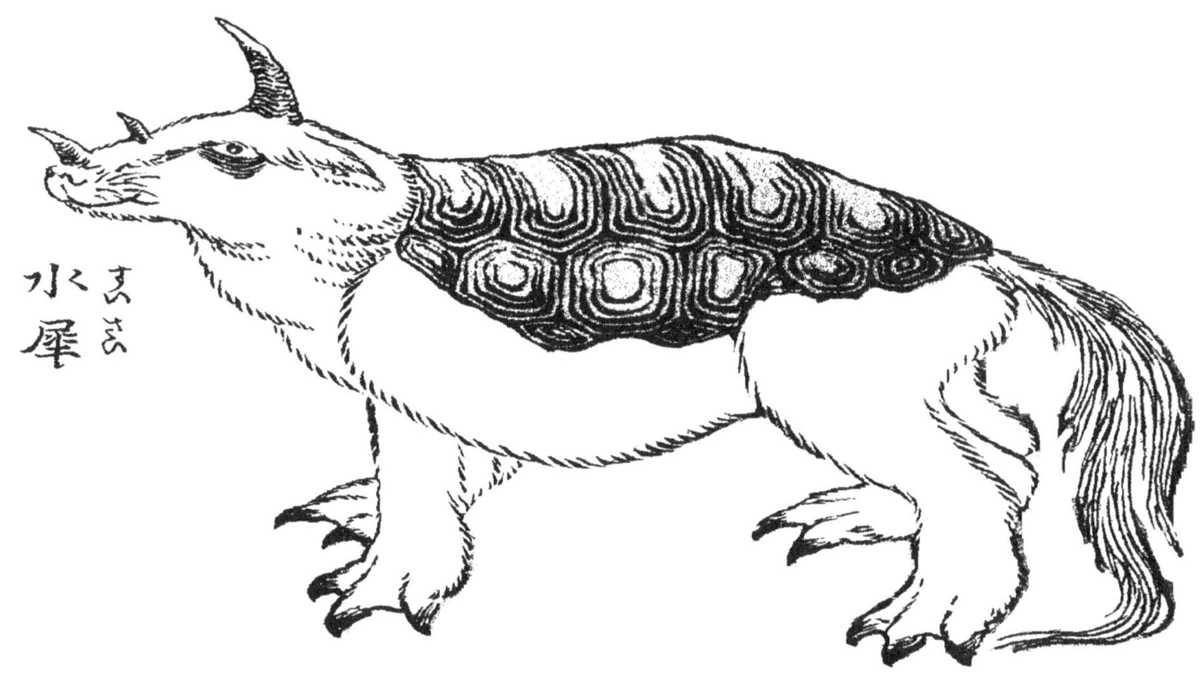

Fable 9   The Boar and the Snake

A boar, which was mercilessly hunted by a pack of hunters, came across a snake, which was sleeping under a bush. "Snake, WHY do you sleep? Hunters are coming! They are going to kill us soon! Flee!"

The snake slowly opened its eyes, and mumbled, "They come for you, not for ME. It is YOU that must flee. We snakes have other problems."

Moral: Wise creatures know how to recognize their own problems.

寓言 9   野猪和蛇

一头野猪被猎人们无情地捕获。它遇到了一条蛇正在灌木丛下睡觉。"蛇，你怎么还在睡觉？猎人们来了！他们很快就会杀了我们！快跑！"

蛇缓缓地睁开眼睛，喃喃地说："他们是来找你的，不是我。是你必须逃离。我们蛇要面对其他的问题。"

寓意：聪明的生物懂得如何识别自己的难题。

Taking It a Step Further ——Moral Prompts

* Are you 'wise enough' to recognize your own problems and not get swept up into other people's issues?

* What would be some reasons to worry about other people's issues and to get involved?

Fable 10   The Sea Lion, the Polar Bear, and the Seal

Because of the lack of cold temperatures, and ice, a sea lion, a polar bear, and a seal were soon caught in a swift current on three ice floes. As the three ice floes twirled and seemingly danced with one another, coming close but not close enough to each other, the three creatures bemoaned their fate as they were pulled further and further out to sea.

Once they lost sight of land, the three called out their fears, but only to have nothing change. The polar bear, which recognized the seriousness of the situation, called out to the sea lion and the seal, "We have to come together, and paddle back to land or we are lost!"

"Are you TRULY crazy?" yelled out the seal. "Once you get close to me, you will have me as a meal. I am truly in dire straits, but I am not stupid."

Moral: A crisis doesn't necessarily mean a change in values or fears.

寓言 10   海狮，北极熊和海豹

由于缺少寒冷的气温和冰，海狮、北极熊和海豹很快被困在三块浮冰上， 周围是湍急的水流。三块浮冰在水里打着转，看起来像是在跳舞。彼此离得不远，可是距离还不够近。看着自己被越来越远地冲向大海深处，三只生物哀叹着自己的命运。

它们终于看不到陆地，于是发出了惊恐的声音，却无能为力去改变。北极熊意识到事态的严重性，对着海狮和海豹喊道："我们必须团结起来，一起划回陆地，否则我们就迷路了！"

"你真地疯了吗？"海豹大喊道。"你一旦靠近我，你就会把我当饭吃掉。我确实是处于可怕的困境，但是我并不傻。"

寓意：危机并不一定意味着恐惧意识的改变。

Taking It a Step Further ——Moral Prompts

* Do you really think that a crisis can change some people's values or fears? In what situations might this be true?

* Has anything bad in your life ever affected your outlook, values or fears?

Fable 11   The Grand Scheme

A large python could barely believe its eyes. There below it sat a large turkey, bathing in the sun, completely oblivious to everything around it. The python's sister soon slithered up next to it and said, "What a prize! This will last us for breakfast, lunch, and dinner, I dare say."

"Yes, but turkeys are not stupid. We have to be smart about this," her brother replied. "You should approach from the front, and I will come from behind. In this way, there is no escape."

"Dear Brother! Our cousins tried this last week with a boar, and guess what, it didn't work! The boar just dashed off to the left and ran away. Every snake does this! Let's try something new! I think we should just 'pop on down from above' so it doesn't see us at all. In this way, we can catch our prize."

Moral: Originality will bring you more gifts.

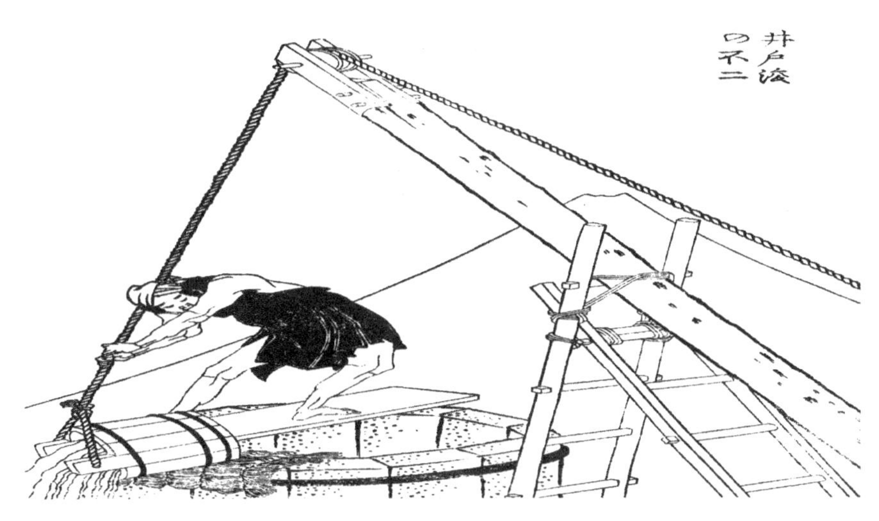

寓言 11　宏伟的计划

一条巨蟒蛇简直不敢相信自己的眼睛。一只超大火鸡坐在下面，正在阳光下沐浴。火鸡对周围的一切毫无察觉。蟒蛇的姐姐很快就爬到它身边，说："多好的奖励！我敢说，这足够我们的早餐、午餐和晚餐了。"

"是的，可是火鸡并不愚蠢。我们必须机灵些。" 她的兄弟回答说。"你从前面靠近，我从后面过来。如此一来，它就无路可逃。"

"亲爱的兄弟！我们的表哥上周对一头野猪试过这个办法。你猜怎么着？一点儿用都没有！野猪冲向左边，然后就跑掉了。每条蛇都选择这样做！让我们尝试一些新方法！我认为我们应该"从上面直接冲下去"，这样它就根本看不到我们。我们就可以拿到我们的奖品。"

寓意：创意会给你带来更多惊喜。

Taking It a Step Further ——Moral Prompts

* Do you think you are an 'original' thinker? If so, how?

* What can you do to be more original than you are now?

Fable 12   The Accusation

A goose and the gander were quarreling. "You cheated on me," blurted out the goose to the gander. The gander was insulted. "ME? CHEAT? Why! I am as pure as the driven snow. I cannot cheat even if I wanted to."

"WELL, WHOSE feathers are those on your backside?" shrieked the goose.

"Oh - those? Those are Frank's. We got into a fight over some small fish."

"Well, what about those wet spots all over your neck? It looks like some goose has been licking you！"

"Those aren't from licking. I was…..standing….beneath Mr. Potter's pipe, and some water dripped on me," replied the gander.

"What about those scratch marks on your legs?"

"Oh—those? I got those…..wading over there in those dense bushes…..along the water's edge," retorted the gander, which was now getting annoyed. "And what about YOU? Where did you get those lick marks? Huh? Huh?"

The goose laughed. "Don't you remember? You gave me those!"

Moral: Accusations are like a double-sided sword: they can cut both ways.

寓言 12 指责

母鹅和公鹅在吵架。"你欺骗了我"，母鹅对公鹅脱口而出。

公鹅被侮辱了。"我？欺骗？我是多么地纯洁无暇！ 即使我想骗你也做不到啊。"

"那，你背后的那些羽毛是谁的？"母鹅尖叫起来。

"哦 -- 那些？是弗兰克的。我们为了一些小鱼打架了。"

"嗯，你脖子上的那些湿漉漉的地方呢？好像是有母鹅亲你了。"

"那不是亲的。我当时……站在……波特先生的水管下面，有些水滴在了我身上"，公鹅回答说。

"那你腿上那些划痕呢？"

"哦 -- 那些？我……在那些茂密的灌木丛中淌水……沿着岸边。"公鹅汇报说。它已经有些恼怒了。"那你呢？你的那些舔痕怎么解释？嗯？嗯？"

母鹅笑了。"你忘了吗？你亲我了！"

寓意：指责就像一把双刃剑，可以向两边切割。

Taking It a Step Further ——Moral Prompts

* Have you ever made any personal accusations and how did that go?

* Have you ever witnessed a married couple accusing each other of something? What was the outcome?

Fable 13　Head North, Head North

A herd of reindeer in the wastelands of Alaska had dwindled in size over the summer due to overhunting by Indians and by the white settlers who were now descending in ever-larger numbers into the area.

The leader of the herd couldn't make up its mind, and upon encountering a white fox, it asked: "Which direction should we go to escape the humans? They are a fearful thing."

The fox shook itself with fear, and replied, "Yes, I have the same problem. They hunt me for my fur. We have to escape to the North."

"But there is nothing there except for some fungi; life is hard and bitterly cold," replied the caribou. "Not to mention the POLAR BEARS!"

"You can die slowly there or die quickly here," sniffed the fox, which then dashed off.

"WELL, THAT was NOT helpful," snorted the reindeer. After a few miles, he encountered a white rabbit, and asked the same question.

The rabbit shook itself with fear, and replied, "Yes, I have the same problem. The people hunt us for our meat and fur. We have to escape to the East."

"But there are so many swamps, and then there are huge mountains. Many of my herd won't make it on this journey," complained the reindeer leader.

"You can die slowly in the mountains or die quickly here," whispered the white rabbit, which then dashed off.

"WELL, THAT was NOT helpful either," snorted the reindeer leader. After a day of traveling, he encountered a mountain goat on a steep hill, and he asked the same question.

The goat shook itself with fear, and replied, "Yes, I have the exact same problem; they hunt us for our meat. We have to escape to the West or to the South."

"But there are so many large rivers in both directions which are impossible to cross, and many bogs which many of our kind get sucked into and never can escape. Many of my herd won't make it on this journey," complained the reindeer.

"You can die quickly in the rivers or slowly of starvation here," whispered the goat, which then slowly eased his way back up the hill.

"THAT was NOT helpful too. WELL, aren't there any creatures HERE that can give ANY GOOD advice around here?" snorted the reindeer.

A young bull reindeer then lumbered up to its leader and laughed, "I think we have run out of directions to escape to, my dear leader."

Moral: Some seek out advice but have no intention of ever taking it.

寓言 13 向北走，向北走

随着越来越多的白人在阿拉斯加地区定居，印第安人和白人开始过度捕猎驯鹿，导致荒地中的驯鹿的数量在夏季急剧减少。

鹿群的首领拿不定主意该怎么办。它遇到了一只白狐，于是问道："我们该往哪个方向走以便躲避人类？他们真是太可怕了。"

狐狸吓得浑身颤抖，回答说："是的，我也有同样的问题。他们为了得到我的毛皮，到处追捕我。我们必须逃到北方去。"

"但那里除了一些菌类什么都没有；生活非常艰难又特别寒冷。"驯鹿回答道，"更不用说还有北极熊了！"

"在那里你可以慢慢死去，可是在这里你会死得很快。"狐狸抽了抽鼻子，然后飞奔而去。

"嗯，真是没用的建议。"驯鹿哼了一声。又走了几英里，它遇到了一只白兔，又问了同样的问题。

兔子吓得浑身颤抖，回答说："是的，我也有同样的问题。人们为了得到我们的肉和毛皮而猎杀我们。我们必须逃到东边去。"

"但是那里有那么多沼泽，还有巨大的山脉。我的鹿群根本无法完成这次旅程。"驯鹿首领抱怨道。

"你可以在山上慢慢地死，也可以在这里死得很快。"白兔小声说道，然后飞奔而去。

"哎，又是一个没用的答案。"驯鹿首领哼了一声。经过了一天的旅行，它在陡峭的山坡上遇到了一只山羊，于是又问了同样的问题。

山羊吓得浑身颤抖，回答说："是的，我也有完全同样的问题。他们想吃我们的肉，于是猎杀我们。我们必须逃到西边或南边。"

"但是，在这两个方向都有太多无法跨越的大河，还有许多沼泽，我们许多驯鹿都会陷入其中，永远无法逃脱。我的鹿群根本无法完成这次旅程。"驯鹿抱怨道。

"你会在河里死得很快，也可以在这里慢慢饿死。" 山羊低声说着，然后慢吞吞地回到了山上。

"这个说法也没有用。好吧，难道这里没有任何生物可以提供好的建议吗？" 驯鹿喷着鼻息。

一只年轻的公驯鹿缓慢笨拙地走到它的首领面前，笑着说，"我想我们已经没有方向可逃了，我亲爱的首领。"

寓意：有些人寻求建议，但却无意接受。

Taking It a Step Further ——Moral Prompts

* Some say that 'advice' is useless as no one ever listens to it. Do you

ever 'take anyone's advice' and if so, on what issues and from whom?

* Do you know of people who are happy to always give advice but never take it?

Fable 14   Glimpses of a River

A large catfish that was on a catfish farm had grown strong and mighty over the past year. In fact, it was now the largest catfish in the entire pool, but the catfish had grown very tired of its surroundings and its companions.

The catfish would time from time jump as high as it could and would think that it would see a river in the distance. Freedom! It would mean landing on the ground, but catfish were no strangers to making it a short distance across some land.

More and more jumps seemed to confirm the initial impression, and the catfish could barely contain itself. "I have to jump! I will be FREE. It's so simple! I will no longer swim around here for the human's pleasure."

The catfish's wife and children looked back at the catfish and wailed, "What about us? What will happen to us? Please don't leave!" At this point, the catfish realized that simply jumping to freedom was no easy matter.

Moral: Those who say 'it's simple,' are simple.

寓言 14　瞥见一条河

在过去的一年里，鲶鱼养殖场的一条大鲶鱼长大，强壮了许多。实际上，它现在是整个池塘中最大的鲶鱼，但是它已经厌倦了周围的环境和同伴。

鲶鱼时不时尽可能高地跳出水面，期待可以看到远处的河流。自由！这可能意味着落在地面上，但鲶鱼坚信它有办法找到比较近的距离穿越陆地。

一次又一次的跳跃似乎印证了它的最初印象，鲶鱼几乎无法克制自己。"我必须跳起来！那才是自由。多简单的事情！我不会再为了人类高兴在这里游来游去。"

鲶鱼的妻儿回头看着鲶鱼，哀号说："那我们呢？我们会发生什么？请不要离开！"这时候，鲶鱼才意识到，单纯地跳向自由并不是一件容易的事。

寓意：总是说"那很简单"的人很幼稚。

Taking It a Step Further ——Moral Prompts

* Do you think often 'minimize problems' and are too optimistic about certain problems and issues?

* Some people are very quick in making decisions while others are quite deliberative and careful? What about you?

Fable 15　The Apes and The Chimpanzees

A group of apes was on the move looking for better food sources. But each time, they found something always lacking. If they found bananas, they could not find water. If they encountered water, there was, more often than not, no bananas or leaves to munch on.

One day, they encountered a large group of chimpanzees. So, the lead ape waddled up to the group and pounded on his chest, demanding to know where the best food supply was.

The chimpanzees knew immediately that apes were creatures that did not share. Not. One. Little. Bit. So, eventually, a 'leader' of the chimpanzees was pushed to the front, and he replied, "The best food supply. Why! It's over by the river. Follow the sun."

The ape smiled and did not reply, leading his band with him, and after a day's march, they came across a city of people. When seeing the ape band, the people got baseball bats and weapons and began going after the apes, all of which had fled back to the forest.

The ape leader was beyond fury and was ready to tear the chimpanzees into pieces, all of which had clambered into the tops of the trees, clinging on to small and large branches.

"HOW DARE YOU LIE TO ME! I AM AN APE OF THE CHOHOE CLAN. NO ONE LIES TO ME," bellowed the ape.

The 'leader' of the chimpanzees, which was again pushed to the forefront of a branch, replied, "You asked about the best food supply.

We told you the TRUTH. The humans have the best food supply. You didn't ask about the safest and the best food supply. It's your own fault."

Moral: Watch out for those who provide simple answers.

寓言 15　类人猿和黑猩猩

一群类人猿正在移动，寻找更好的食物来源。可是每一次，他们总是发现缺少一些什么。如果他们发现了香蕉，就找不到水。如果他们遇到了水源，通常不会有香蕉或树叶供它们咀嚼。

有一天，他们遇到了一大群黑猩猩。于是，领头的类人猿摇摇晃晃地走到黑猩猩们面前，拍打着自己的胸口，询问哪里才有最好的食物供应。

黑猩猩们立刻意识到，类人猿是不会分享的生物。不，绝对不。一个也不行，很少也不行。于是，最终，领头的黑猩猩被推到了前面。他回答说："最好的食物供应。哦，就在河边啊。它跟着太阳走。"

类人猿笑着没有搭话。而是带着一行人，经过一天的奔波，遇到了一群人。当看到类人猿们，人们纷纷拿起棒球棒和武器，开始追击它们。于是所有的类人猿又逃回了森林。

领头的类人猿怒不可遏，准备将黑猩猩们撕成碎片。黑猩猩们已经全都爬到了树上，紧紧抓着大大小小的树枝。

"你们怎么敢骗我！我是乔霍氏族的类人猿。没有人对我说谎。"类人猿生气地吼叫着。

领头的黑猩猩再次被推到了一个靠前的树枝上。它回答说："你问我们哪有最好的食物供应。我们告诉了你真相。人类拥有最好的食物。你并没有问我们最安全和最好的食物供应。是你自己的错。"

寓意：小心提防那些提供简单答案的人。

Taking It a Step Further ——Moral Prompts

* Do you listen and just respond to 'an answer or directions' without asking a lot of questions?

* The ape leader was rather naïve and trusting. Do you see yourself in this way?

Fable 16   The Cobra and the Snake Charmer

A cobra was captured by a snake charmer one day and was used in a snake show. The charmer would play a flute, and the cobra would slither out and would raise itself, flowing this way and that to the tune of the music. The audience laughed and laughed.

One day, when the snake charmer was taking a train, the cobra was placed on the train platform beside some other snakes, which were to be placed in a zoo.

Upon hearing about the cobra's life, the snakes mocked it mercilessly. "Are you NOT a COBRA, one of the deadliest snakes that crawl on this earth? Teach this fool a lesson and bite him the next time he tries to charm you," they chorused.

"Well, I am not sure if he deserves THAT. He does feed me well. And the music is pretty good!" This reply was met with a hail of laugher and insults.

"Are you MAD? Have you lost your common sense, your identity? BITE HIM! Show him no mercy!" hissed the group of snakes before they were thrown on to train compartment.

The cobra was now perplexed and confused. What to do? It then decided that identity was more important than music and food. So, it decided to bite the snake charmer, the next time there was a show.

When the music started, however, the cobra slithered up and waved back and forth with the music, it completely forgot about its plans and danced with the music, and did so for the rest of its life.

Moral: Music can soothe the most savage of beasts.

寓言 16　眼镜蛇和耍蛇人

一天，一只眼镜蛇被耍蛇人捕获，并被用来进行一场耍蛇表演。耍蛇人吹奏长笛，眼镜蛇就会蜿蜒着身体慢慢滑出，然后高高升起，随着音乐的节奏来回摇摆。观众们哈哈大笑。

一天，耍蛇人乘坐火车的时候，眼镜蛇被放在了火车的月台上。旁边还有一些其他的蛇，它们是要被放到动物园里。

听说了眼镜蛇的生活，其他的蛇都无情地嘲笑它。"你难道不是地球上最最致命的眼镜蛇吗？给这个傻瓜一个教训，下次他试图引诱你的时候，咬他一口。"他们齐声说。

"嗯，我并不确定是否应该那样做。他把我喂养得很好，而且音乐也很好听！"这个回答引来了一阵嘲笑和侮辱。

"你疯了吗？你已经失去了你的常识，你的身份吗？咬他！不要怜悯他！"这群蛇在被扔进火车车厢之前，发出了嘶嘶的声音。

眼镜蛇现在感到茫然和困惑。该怎么办？随后它决定，自己的身份比音乐和食物更重要。所以，它决定下次有表演的时候，就去咬一下耍蛇人。

然而，当音乐响起，眼镜蛇爬了起来，随着音乐的节拍来回舞动身体。它完全忘记了自己的计划，随着音乐翩翩起舞。就这样，它度过了自己的余生。

寓意：音乐可以抚慰最野蛮的野兽。

Taking It a Step Further ——Moral Prompts

* Do think music can change your own plans about something?

* How important is music to your own life?

Fable 17   The Wolf and the Shepherd

One day a wolf, upon seeing an inexperienced and young shepherd, approached him and boldly said, "Look, you are too innocent to work here. I can cause GREAT damage, UNLESS…..say….you give me a nice pot of stewed meat -- every day. If you do so, then I will leave you and worthless flock to yourselves. Fail to do this, many of your sheep will be hauled away and mauled to death. Maybe I might even get to YOU!"

The young shepherd was near to tears and complained to his father, who then had a plan. "Ok, give him this pot of stew tomorrow. Sometimes the strong are just too strong for us. Know when to bend."

The young shepherd met the wolf the next day, bowed, and offered the pot of stew that was greedily eaten up. "You have done well, young shepherd. Keep up the good work and tomorrow, add some milk to this. I like milk!" With that, the wolf dashed off to the forest.

When the young shepherd returned that evening and told the father that the wolf had eaten the stew and wanted some more tomorrow along with some milk, the father laughed and laughed.

"You don't EVER have to worry about that wolf again, my son. He is now probably dying a painful death. I poisoned that stew. There is no way, he is going to make it tomorrow to bother us again. As I said, it is important to know when to bow and when not to. This was not our time to bow, much less to a stupid and arrogant wolf."

Moral: Bullies often interpret signs of fear and obedience with stupidity, thus allowing them to be easily trapped.

寓言 17　狼和牧羊人

一天，狼看到了一个没有经验的年轻的牧羊人，于是走近他，大胆地说："哎，你太天真了，不能在这里工作。我可以造成巨大的麻烦，除非……比如说……你每天给我一罐美味的炖肉。如果你这样做，那么我会离开你和毫无价值的羊群。如果不这样做，你的许多只羊将会被拖走撕碎。可能你也不能幸免！"

年轻的牧羊人几乎要哭了，对他的父亲抱怨着。他的父亲有了一个计划。"哦，明天把这锅炖肉给他。有时候，强者对我们来说实在太强大了。要知道什么时候该弯腰。"

第二天，年轻的牧羊人遇见了狼。他鞠了一躬，将一锅炖肉给了狼。狼贪婪地吃光了。"你做得很好，年轻的牧羊人。保持住良好的工作状态。明天，加一些牛奶在里面。我喜欢牛奶！"说完，狼就跑回了森林。

那天晚上，年轻的牧羊人回家告诉他的父亲，狼吃光了炖肉，第二天还要吃一些，而且要加牛奶。他的父亲开心地笑了。

"你再也不用担心那只狼了，我的儿子。他现在可能正在痛苦地死去。我在那个炖肉里下了毒。没办法，不这样做，他就会来找我们的麻烦。正如我所说，重要的是要知道什么时候该弯腰，什么时候不。这不是我们需要弯腰的时候，对愚蠢傲慢的狼，更不能。"

寓意：霸凌经常诠释着恐惧的信号和愚蠢的服从，从而让霸凌者落入陷阱。

Taking It a Step Further ——Moral Prompts

* Have you ever been bullied? How did you solve the problem?

* Do you think you should ever show 'fear' to a bully? What is the

best way to respond to someone that tries to dominate you?

Fable 18   The Coyote

A coyote walking along a mountain path saw a young calf from a nearby ranch injured. The coyote turned and looked at the ranch to see a human running as fast as he could to where the two were.

The coyote noted to itself, "No matter how well I might explain that I had nothing to do with this, I would never be believed." And so, with that in mind, he took the calf and as fast as possible, he dragged it back up the mountain out of reach of the rancher.

Moral: Explanations are of little use to those who refuse to listen.

寓言 18　土狼

一只土狼沿着山路行走。它看到附近牧场的一头小牛受伤了。土狼转过身凝视牧场，看到一个人正以最快的速度跑向它们两个所在的地方。

土狼自言自语说："无论我怎么解释说我与此事无关，没有人会相信我。"想到这里，于是，它带着小牛，以最快的速度，把它拖回了牧场主到不了的山上。

寓意：对于拒绝倾听的人，解释毫无用处。

Taking It a Step Further ——Moral Prompts

* Have you ever tried to explain yourself to someone but they were ever in the mind to listen to you?

*Do you often find that older people rarely listen to you? Who are ones, however, that do pay attention to what you have to say?

Fable 19　Explaining the Crocodile

One day, some crabs, oysters, and clams were discussing how something as hideous as crocodiles could exist. The crab straddled up and said, that the crocodile exists to keep the oysters and clams in check, by stepping on them. "It's because of you creatures, that we are vexed by this monster. You keep trying to rise above your station!"

The oysters and clams were outraged. "We are often in too deep water for the crocodiles to step on us. It is because of your habits of leaving bits of food here and there. It attracts them."

"Well, arguing about this isn't going to solve the problem of crocodile removal. One of us has to do it," replied the crabs.

With that, both the oysters and clams clambered back into the sand, and to this day, no creature even thinks about bothering the crocodile.

Moral: Passivity allows monsters to roam freely.

寓言 19　有关鳄鱼的解释

有一天，一些螃蟹、牡蛎和蛤蜊正在讨论怎么会有像鳄鱼这样可怕的东西存在。螃蟹横起了身子说，鳄鱼的存在就是为了控制牡蛎和蛤蜊，踩在它们头上。"就是因为你们这些生物，我们才被这个怪物烦扰。你们一直试图超越你们的身份！"

牡蛎和蛤蜊被激怒了。"我们经常在很深的水里，鳄鱼根本无法踩到我们。这是因为你的习惯，到处留一些食物，它才被吸引。"

"嗯，争论这个问题并不能解决怎样除掉鳄鱼这个麻烦。我们中的一人必须行动。"螃蟹回答道。

听到这句话，牡蛎和蛤蜊都爬回到沙子里。直到今天，没有任何生物有想法要去打扰鳄鱼。

寓意：被动让怪兽放逸横行。

Taking It a Step Further ——Moral Prompts

* Do you see yourself as passive or do you take an active role in improving your local community and society in some fashion?

* What kinds of problems in society worry you and provoke you to want to speak out?

Fable 20   The Dolphin and the Boat

One day a lonely dolphin spied a large boat and was greatly impressed as to how it plowed through the ocean. The dolphin raced to it and jumped in its wake. The dolphin tried talking to it several times, but the boat kept a strange and mysterious silence, which intrigued the dolphin even more.

"Such a mighty beast such as this is too busy for words and must be the king of the ocean. I will follow it wherever it goes." Some of the other dolphins caught up to it, but soon lost interest in the boat and went their own way.

Eventually, the boat made its way into a harbor where it stopped and churned out black smoke and diesel fumes. The dolphin looked around at the other boats sitting quietly in the harbor and soon realized that the boat was nothing to adore or to follow.

Moral: Followers should know that their leaders might often take them nowhere.

寓言 20　海豚和船

有一天，一只孤独的海豚看到了一艘大船，对于它如何在海洋中航行留下了深刻的印象。海豚快速游到大船旁边，跟在船后边跳跃。海豚多次尝试和它交谈，但是大船始终保持着诡异而神秘的沉默，这让海豚更加好奇。

"如此威武的猛兽，忙得连说话的时间都没有，它一定是海洋之王。无论它走到哪里，我都会追随它。"其他一些海豚也跟了上来，但很快就对大船失去了兴趣而走开了。

最终，这艘船驶进了一个港口，在那里停了下来，冒着黑烟和柴油的臭气。海豚环顾四周，看到其他船只静静地停泊在港口里，很快就意识到这艘大船没有什么值得崇拜和追随的。

寓意：追随者应该明白他们的领导者可能最终不会成功。

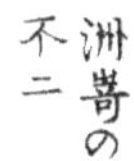

Taking It a Step Further ——Moral Prompts

* Do you know of any leaders who have done very little for your country but have made many 'fine speeches' and had received a lot of attention?

* Have you ever been impressed by someone only to learn later on that he or she didn't earn your respect?

Fable 21   The Cormorant and the Fisherman

One day a Japanese fisherman caught a young cormorant. It wasn't long afterward that the fisherman put a tight metal ring around the bird's throat. As the cormorant dived and caught a fish, the bird found that it could not swallow the fish. What was worse, the fisherman would take away the fish without a word of thanks.

After a few days of diving and having the fisherman repeated take its fish away, the fisherman seized the bird and put it in a cage, removed the ring, and then fed it just two fish. That night, after the fisherman had gone to his house, the bird asked the other cormorants what to do about this situation.

"I dive all day long, and I should have had 50 fish to eat, and he gives me only two. It's not fair!" complained the young cormorant.

"Ah," said an older cormorant, "of course, the fisherman benefits immensely from our work. But if we were to flee and fly away, we would starve with these rings around our necks. Therefore, we have to be content with the little that we have; there is just no other option for us cormorants."

Moral: Cruelty is always rationalized away.

寓言 21　鸬鹚和渔夫

一天，一位日本渔民捕获了一只幼小的鸬鹚。不久之后，渔夫就在鸟的喉咙处套上了一个紧密的金属环。当鸬鹚潜入水中叼到鱼时，它发现自己无法吞下这条鱼。更糟糕的是，渔夫一句话也不说就把鱼拿走了。

经过了几天的潜水，渔夫一次又一次地鱼拿走。最后渔夫抓住了这只鸟，把它关在笼子里，取下了金属环，然后只喂给它两条鱼。那天晚上，渔夫回家了，鸬鹚询问其他的伙伴该如何处理这种情况。

"我潜水一整天，我应该有 50 条鱼吃，可是他只给了我两条。这不公平！"年幼的鸬鹚抱怨道。

"哦，"一位年长的鸬鹚说，"当然，渔夫从我们的工作中获得巨大利益。但是，如果我们逃跑飞走，我们会因为脖子上的金属环而饿死。所以，我们必须满足于我们所拥有的，虽然很少。作为鸬鹚，我们别无选择。"

寓意：残忍总是被合理化。

Taking It a Step Further ——Moral Prompts

* Have you seen or experienced people who 'rationalized' or 'explained away' particularly difficult rules or extremely high standards?

* What kinds of people, do you think, are the most cruel?

Fable 22   The Tasmanian Devil's Mask

A starving Tasmanian devil was searching the forest for food. The problem was that as soon as it saw food, the "food" also saw it, and ran quickly away, shrieking out its terror. This also scared away all other "food" and made things worse!

"I think that I have an image problem," the Tasmanian devil said to itself. "I look too serious." And when looking upon its reflection in a lake, the devil was even more surprised. "Why I look like a hideous terrorist. Almost as bad as a human! No wonder all of my food is fleeing from me! I must do something about my image."

The Tasmanian devil searched around and found a dead kangaroo. After some work, the devil managed to take off the head and most of its fur. It then used this head as a large 'mask.'

As the devil walked….or staggered through the forest in its new disguise, it found that this mask was far worse. Not only could the devil not see, but also even more creatures fled at the sight of a kangaroo head moving through the forest floor.

Moral: A mask rarely covers up one's true character or intent.

寓言 22　袋獾的面具

一只饥饿的袋獾在森林里寻找食物。问题是，它一看到食物，"食物"也看到了它，于是飞快地跑开，发出恐怖的尖叫声。这也同时吓跑了所有其他"食物"，让事情变得更糟！

"我认为我的形象有问题，"袋獾对自己说。"我看起来太严肃了。"当它看到湖里自己的倒影，袋獾更是惊讶。"怎么会这样！我看起来像一个可怕的恐怖分子。几乎和人类一样糟糕！难怪我所有的食物都在逃离我！我必须对我的形象进行改进。"

袋獾四处搜寻，发现了一只死去的袋鼠。经过一番努力，袋獾设法取下了它的头和大部分皮毛。然后它把这个头部当作一个大"面具"。

当袋獾戴着新的伪装走着或是蹒跚穿过森林时，它发现这个面具要更加糟糕。袋獾不仅看不见，甚至有更多的生物跑开，因为它们看到一个有袋鼠脑袋的怪物居然穿梭在森林的地面上。

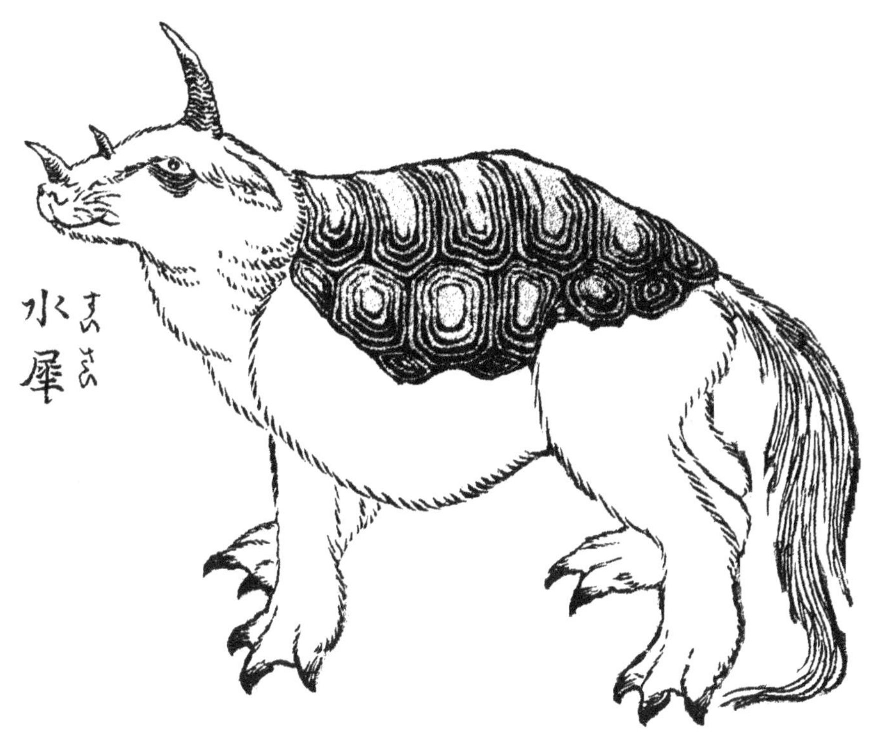

寓意：面具很少能掩盖一个人的真实性格或意图。

Taking It a Step Further -- Moral Prompts

* Do you see people who are not kind often having 'plastic smiles'— which is kind of a mask? How do you recognize a real smile from a fake one?

* Can you still recognize a bad person who is very well dressed? If so, how

Biography

About the Author

Robert Long has lived and worked in Japan for 28 years. He grew up in Florida and graduated from the University of Florida and Florida State University, with a Specialist Degree in Multilingual and Multicultural Education. He has traveled extensively and has worked at Kyushu Institute of Technology for the past 26 years, where he is a professor. His interests include jogging, gardening, art, yoga, and literature.

About the Editor/Translator

Rong Zhang has been teaching both English and for more than 25 years. She obtained her Master degree of English Language Teaching from Fukuoka University of Education, Japan and Ph. D in Engineering from Waseda University, Japan. She has experience of teaching at ten universities in both Japan and China, and is currently teaching at Nishinippon Institute of Technology in Japan as a professor. ......

Art

The manga is from Hokusai, 1997 Master Graphique CD-Rom Anthology.